CAR
SURGERY

EDWARD LEE

deadite
press

deadite press

DEADITE PRESS
205 NE BRYANT
PORTLAND, OR 97211
www.DEADITEPRESS.com

AN ERASERHEAD PRESS COMPANY
www.ERASERHEADPRESS.com

ISBN: 1-936383-49-7

All stories © 2011 by Edward Lee

Cover art copyright © 2011 Alan M. Clark
www.ALANMCLARK.com

Printed in the USA.

CONTENTS

THE SEEKER

Bock's eyes flicked up. "Something buzzing the hopper, Sarge."

Balls, SFC John Ruben thought. He unlocked the alert safe behind the driver's compartment and removed the CEIC binder which contained today's prefixes and code dailies.

Then: "Victor Echo Two Six, this is X-ray One. Acknowledge."

Bock stalled over the radio and AN/FRA shift-converter. "Who the fuck's X-ray One, Sarge? Division?"

Ruben checked the codebook. "It's Air Force Recovery Alert Operations. Gonna get shit on by fly boys again. Answer it."

"X-ray One, this is Victor Echo Two Six. Go ahead."

"Proceed to incoming grid. Target perimeter positive."

Bock held the mike away from himself like a chunk of rancid meat.

Ruben could not believe what he'd just heard. The pause hovered in static, then Ruben grabbed the mike. "X-ray One, this is Victor Echo Two Six Tango Charlie. Repeat your last transmission."

"Proceed to incoming grid," the radio answered back. "Target perimeter positive."

His memory struggled with the reality of fright. The sequence seemed miles away. "Status white. Progress code?"

"Red."

"Recall code?"

"None."

"Directive order?"

"Directive order is standby at target perimeter. This is NOT a drill. This is NOT an exercise. Assume SECMAT alert state orange."

"Orders logged," Ruben droned. *Holy mother of shit,* he thought.

"Victor Echo Two Six, this is X-ray One. Out."

Ruben hung up the AN's mike. Bock was sweating. Jones, the track's driver, craned back from the t-bar. "What gives, Sarge!"

"Calm down," Ruben eased. But he could not calm the thought: *This has never happened before.*

"We're at war," Bock muttered.

The alert had sounded at 0412; they'd been in the field nearly a day now. Victor Echo Two Six was a modified M2 armored personnel carrier, fully CBN equipped, and its crew was what the U.S. Army Chemical Corps termed a hazmat field detection team. Their primary general search perimeter was familiar open scrubby land; they'd tracked this terrain dozens of times on past alerts. Ruben, the TC, hadn't been worried until now—until he'd heard the magic words: *Target perimeter positive.*

"What are you guys, a bunch of dickheads?" he countered. "This is a CONUS alert. If we were at war, the whole state would be a clusterfuck by now, and the op stat would've been jerked up a lot higher than a CONUS. We'd be at Defcon Two at least. Think with your brains instead of your asses. If this was war, why would they recall every unit in the division except us?"

"This is shit, Sarge!" Jones was not appeased. "Something's really fucked up!"

"Calm down. We're not at war."

Bock was shaking, muttering, "It fucking figures. I'm two weeks short, and this shit happens."

"You guys are shitting your pickles for nothing. We had four of these last year, remember? One of the early warning sites probably picked up something in our telemetry line. It's probably another meteor, or a piece of space junk. Relax, will you?"

"Here it comes," Bock announced.

The XN/PCD 21 began to click. The hopper freqs shifted through their 5-digit discriminators. Then the mobile printer spat out their destination grid.

Bock slid out the map book, teeth chattering. Jones' face was turning to paste. They were just boys, and they were shit-scared, but Ruben had to wonder if he was too.

He put his hands on their shoulders. "We gotta get our shit together, girls. We're hardcore Army decon ass-kickers, and we don't piss in our BDU's every time an alert directive goes up. We ain't afraid of nothin'. We eat napalm for breakfast and piss diesel fuel, and when we die and go to hell, we're gonna shove the devil's head up his ass and take the fuck over. Right now we gotta job to do, and I gotta know if you guys are with me."

Bock wiped sweat off his brow with his sleeve. "Hardcore, Sarge. I'm no pussy. My shit's tight, and I'm with you."

"Jonesy?"

Jones gave the thumbs up. "Hell on fucking wheels, man! Nobody lives forever, so let's roll!"

"Hardcore," Ruben approved. "Squared-fucking-away goddamn die-for-decon outstanding."

"Let's kick ass!" Bock yelled.

"Decon!" Jones chanted.

Ruben handed Jones the grid. "Get this twin-tracked Detroit coffin rolling, Jonesy. Hammer down."

Jones revved the throttle, whooping. The track's turbocharged Cummins V8 roared. Bock strapped in behind the commo gear. Ruben had enlivened them, but for how long? What was happening out there? *What's waiting for us?* he wondered.

"Proceed to target perimeter positive," he said.

How powerful is the power of truth?
It was more a motto than a question. It was all that motivated him.

The writer didn't believe in God, for instance. Now, if he *saw* God, then he'd believe in Him. He believed in nothing he couldn't see, but that's why he was here, wasn't it? To see? Behind him, the bus disappeared into darkness. *I see that,* he thought.

Ahead, the sign blazed in blue neon: CROSSROADS.

"I see that, too. A drink, to help me think."

But then he heard a word, or thought he did. It was not his voice, nor a thought of his own. He heard it in his head: SUSTENANCE.

So he was hearing voices now? Perhaps he'd been drinking too much. Or, *Not enough,* he considered, half-smiling. *All great writers drink.* He could not dispel the notion, however, that he was entering something more than just a small-town tavern.

Dust eddied from the wood floor's seams when he trod in and set down his bag. Yes, here was a real "slice of life" bar: a dump. Its frowziness, its cheap tables, dartboards, pinball machines—its overall *Vacuus spiritum*—delighted him. This was reality, and reality was what he sought.

Seek, he thought, *and ye shall find.*

"Welcome to Crossroads, stranger," greeted the rube barkeep. The writer mused over the allegorical possibilities of the bar's name. The keep had a basketball beer belly and teeth that would compel an oral hygienist to consider other career options. "What can I get ya?" he asked.

"Alcohol. Impress me with your mixological prowess, sir."

Only three others graced these eloquent confines. A sad-faced guy in a white shirt sat beside a short, bosomed redhead. They seemed to be arguing. Closer up sat an absolutely obese woman with long blond hair, drinking dark beer and eating an extra-large pizza. Her weight caused the stool's legs to visibly bend.

You're here to seek, the writer reminded himself. *So seek.*

"May I join you?"

The blonde swallowed, nodding. "You ain't from around here."

"No," the writer said, and sat. Then the keep slapped a shooter down. It was yellow. "House special, stranger."

It looked like urine. "What *is* it?"

"We call it the Piss Shooter."

The writer's brow rose. "It's not, uh . . . *piss,* is it?"

The keep laughed. "'Course not! It's vodka and Galliano."

The writer sniffed. *Smells all right.* "Okay, here's to—what? Ah, yes. Here's to formalism." He drank it down.

"Well?"

"Not bad. Very good, actually." He reached for his wallet.

"Uh-uh, stranger. That there's a tin roof."

"What?"

The keep rolled his eyes. "It's on the house."

"What'cha want in a dull's-shit town like this?" inquired the fat blonde, chewing. Her breasts were literally large as human heads. "Ain't nothin' around for fifty miles in any direction."

Isolatus proximus. "I'm a writer," the writer said. "I travel all over the country. I need to see different things, different people. I need to see life in its different temporal stratas."

"Stratas," the fat blonde said, nodding.

"I come to remote towns like this because they're variegated. They exist separately from the rest of the country's societal mainstream. Towns like this are more *real.* I'm a writer, but in a more esoteric sense . . . I'm . . ." He thought about this. He thought hard. He lit a cigarette and finished. "I'm a seeker."

"You've got to be shitting me!" the guy in the white shirt shouted to the short red-haired girl. "You've slept with FIVE OTHER GUYS this week? Jeeeeesus CHRIST!"

She sipped her Tequila Moonrise reflectively, then corrected, "Sorry. Not five. Six. I forgot about Craig." She grinned. "His nickname's Mr. Meat Missile."

"Jeeeeesus CHRIST!" White shirt exploded.

"He must be in love with her," the writer remarked.

"He don't get her pussy off," the fat blonde said.

The keep was polishing a glass. "What's that you were sayin'? You're a *seeker?*"

"Well, that's an abstraction, of course. What I mean is I'm on a quest. I'm searching for some elusive uncommon denominator to perpetuate my aesthetic ideologies. For a work of fiction to exist within any infrastructure of resolute meaning, its peripheries must reflect certain elements of truth. I don't mean objective truths. I'm talking about ephemeral things: *unconscious* impulses, *psychological* propensities, etc.—the *underside* of what we think of as the human experience."

"I've never heard such shit in my life!" White Shirt was still yelling at the redhead. "Those other guys don't love you! *I* love you!"

The redhead doodled indifferently on a napkin. "But I don't want to be loved," she said. Then she grinned as intensely as an Indian devil mask. "I just want to be fucked."

"*Jeeeeeeesus Chriiiiiiiiiiiiiist!*"

"You gotta tune 'em out," advised the fat blonde, now halfway done with the pizza and starting her third dark beer. Grease glossed her lips and chin.

"The seeker," said the keep. "I like that."

"But what exactly do you write about?" asked the blonde.

"*What* I write about isn't the point, it's *how* I write about it." And then, with no warning, the thought returned: *How powerful is the power of truth?* The writer smoked his cigarette deep. "Honesty is the vehicle of my aesthete. The truth of fiction can only exist in its bare words. Pardon my obtuseness, but it's the *mode,* the *application* of the vision which must transcend the overall tangibilities. Prose mechanics, I mean—the structural manipulation of syntactical nomenclatures in order to affect particularized transpositions of imagery."

"Oh," said the fat blonde. "I thought you meant, like, fucking'n shit like that."

The writer frowned.

He swigged another Piss Shooter, another tin roof. The fat blonde's pizza lay thick with extra cheese, anchovies, and big chunks of sausage beneath a sheen of grease. Her stomach made fish tank noises as she voraciously ate and drank.

"Why, why, why?" White Shirt looked close to tears, or a schizoaffective episode, staring at the redhead. "At least tell me why I'm not good enough anymore?"

"You don't want to know," she nonchalantly replied.

White Shirt hopped off his stool to stalk around her. Anger made his face appear corrugated. "Go ahead! Tell me! Spit it out! I WANT TO KNOW!"

The redhead shrugged. "Your dick's not big enough."

Oh, dear, thought the writer.

White Shirt's low moan issued out like that of a just-gelded walrus. He stumbled away crosseyed, and staggered out of the bar.

11

The keep and fat blonde ignored the outburst. The redhead looked at the writer, smiled, and said, "Hey, he wanted the truth, so I gave it to him."

Truth, thought the writer. Suddenly, he felt empty, desolate.

"But if you're a seeker," posed the keep, "What'cha seekin'?"

"Ah, the universal question." The writer raised a finger, as if to preamble a scintillating wisdom. "And the answer is this. The true seeker never knows what he's seeking until he finds it."

The fat blonde's wet eating noises ceased; she'd finished the entire pizza. "Here's something for you to write about," she said. She leaned over and kissed the writer on the mouth.

Her lips tasted of grease and cheese. But actually the kiss inspired him. Her mouth opened and closed over his, tongue probing unabashed. The writer found himself growing aroused.

Truth, he thought frivolously. *Ephemeral reality.* This was it, wasn't it? Spontaneous human interface, inexplicably complex yet baldly simple. Synaptic and chemical impulses of the brain meshed with someone's lifetime of learned behavior. It was these simple truths that he lived for. They nourished him. *Human truth is my sustenance,* he thought, and remembered the voice he'd heard. Yes, sustenance.

The fat blonde's kiss grew ravenous. Then—

urrrrrrp

She threw up directly into the writer's mouth.

It had come in a single, heaving gust. He tasted everything: warm beer, lumps of half digested sausage and pizza dough, and bile—lots of bile. Utter disgust bulged his eyes and seized his joints. Then came a second, and larger, gust, which she projected right into his lap.

The writer fell off his stool.

"There," said the blonde. "Write about that."

"Ooooo-eee!" remarked the keep. "That one was a doozy, huh?"

The writer, flat on his back and in shock, could only groan, staring up. The heavy, hot blanket of vomit lay thick from chin to crotch; it oozed down his legs slow as lava when he got up. He spat immediately, of course, and incessantly, and out flew several chunks of sausage and strings of flecked slime. Almost blind, he staggered for the door.

"Come again . . . seeker," laughed the keep.

"Hope you liked the pizza," bid the fat blonde.

The writer grabbed his suitcase and stumbled out. The dusk in the sky had bled to full dark, and it was hot outside. He reeked, drenched. He was mortified. *Human truth is my sustenance?* he thought. *Jesus.* The awful tinge in his mouth seemed to buzz, and he could still taste the sausage.

Then he heard the voice again, not in his ears, in his head. What was it?

He stood stock-still in the empty street, sopped in vomit.

SEEKER, said the voice. SEEK AND YE SHALL FIND.

The power of truth? He'd come here seeking truth and all he'd gotten was puked on. And he was hearing voices, too. *Great,* he thought. *Fantastic.* But he had to find a motel, get showered and changed.

He strayed up the main drag, aimless. Shops were closed, houses were dark. The bus station was closed too, and in his wandering he found not one motel.

Then he saw the church.

It sat back quaintly behind some trees, its clean white walls lambent in the night. What relieved him was that it looked *normal.* The front doors stood open and, within, candles could be seen.

He entered and crossed the nave. The pews were empty.

Ahead, past the chancel, a shadow lingered, mumbling low words like an incantation.

It was a priest, reading rites before an open coffin.

"Excuse me, father," the writer said. "I need to know—"

The priest turned, chubby in black raiments. He was glaring. In the coffin lay the corpse of an old woman.

"What!"

"I'm new in town. Are there any motels?"

"Motels? Here?" the priest snapped. "Of course not!"

The writer's eyes flicked to the open coffin. "Do you by chance know when the next bus arrives?"

"How dare you come in here now!" the priest outraged. He pointed abruptly to the coffin. "Can't you see my mother's died?"

"Sorry, father," the writer groped but thought, *God!* He hurried back out. In the street he felt strange, not desolate as before, but woozy, disconnected. *Is it the town, or is it me?* A sudden and profuse flash of sweat made his vomit-drenched shirt feel like a coat of mucus.

The sweat was a herald, like a trumpet—

Oh, no.

—for the voice:

SEEKER. SEEK!

A block down, the sign glowed over the transom: POLICE. His footsteps echoed round his head like a halo as he trotted up. Surely the police would know about the next bus. He pushed through the door, was about to speak, but froze.

A big cop with chopburns glared at him. "What'cha want, buddy? I'm busy."

"I . . ." the writer attempted. The cop was busy, all right. He stood behind a long-haired kid who'd been handcuffed to a chair. A tourniquet had been fashioned about the kid's neck via a cord and nightstick.

"Okay, punk," warned the cop. "No more bullshit. Where's them drugs?"

The kid, of course, couldn't have answered if he'd wanted to. He was being choked. The mouth moved in panic within the strained, ballooning face.

"Still not talkin', huh?" The cop gave the tourniquet another twist.

"What the hell are you doing?" shouted the writer.

"Police business. This kid's got drugger written all over him. Sells the shit to kindergarten kids probably. All that crack and PCP, you now? We gotta rough 'em up a little; it's the only way to get anything out of 'em."

Rough them up a little? The writer stared, flabbergasted. The cop twisted the tourniquet all the way down, until the cord creaked. The kid's body stiffened up in the chair, his face turning blue.

"Talk, punk. Where's your stash? Who's your bagman?"

"How can he talk!" the writer shouted the logical question. "You've got a tourniquet around his fucking neck!"

"Scram, buddy. This is a police matter." The cop paused and looked down. "Aw, shit, there he went." The kid twitched a few times, then fell limp, swollen-faced in death.

Madness, the writer thought.

The cop was unwinding the tourniquet, taking off the cuffs. "Just a drugger, no loss. No point in wastin' it, either." The cop gave the writer a comradely look. "Girl pussy, boy pussy, s'all pink on the inside, right, buddy? Help me get his pants off so's we can poke him 'fore he's cold."

A sign on the wall read *To Protect and Serve.* The writer, brain thumping, teetered out of the station.

Phone, he thought dumbly. He abandoned his suitcase in the street and staggered on. *Something's happened here. Got to call someone, get some help.* The houses set back off the street looked harmless. He knocked on the first door. A middle-aged man answered it—

"Yes? Can I help you, young man?"

"I . . ." the writer attempted. The man wore eyeshadow and cherry-red lipstick. He also wore panties, garters, and stockings. Stainless-steel clamps were screwed down on his nipples, distending the fleshy ends.

"Sporty, wouldn't you say?"

"Huh?"

The man lowered his frilled panties, revealing a penis and scrotum glittery with safety pins. One pin pinched closed the end of the foreskin.

"Uh . . . sporty, yes," the writer said.

"Would you care to touch it?"

"Uh, well, no—"

The writer jogged off. At the second house he peered through the storm door and saw a beautiful nude woman chasing a giant St. Bernard, and a man at the third house stood grinning on his porch rail, a noose around his neck. "Fly, Fleance! Fly," he quoted Shakespeare, and stepped off the rail. Heavy, tonerous thuds greeted the writer at the fourth house. *WHACK-WHACK-WHACK! WHACK-WHACK-WHACK!* In the kitchen window, he saw a man very contentedly cracking open a baby's head with a large meat tenderizer while an aproned woman prepared a fry pan in the background. The man pried the cranium apart and began to spoon the tender brains into a bowl. "Olive oil or canola?" the man asked the wife.

The writer foundered away, gagging, and tripped back into the street. The impact of vision made him feel sledgehammered in the face. He'd seen enough; he didn't want to be a seeker anymore—he just wanted to go home. Then the sweat rushed again, and the voice, like a raddled chord, fell back into his head:

BUT THERE'S SO MUCH, SO MUCH FOR US TO SEEK.

Whatever did that mean? Without reservation, the writer bent over and threw up. This seemed the logical thing to do, an obligation, in fact, after all he'd seen. *Madness,* he repeated, urping it up spasm after spasm like a human sludge-pump. Ropes of saliva dangled off his lips as his stomach rocketed out its contents. The wet splattering crackled down the street.

Oh, what a day.

Done, he felt worse, he felt decamped. The particulate mush of his last meal glittered nearly jewel-like in the frosty glow of streetlamps. He felt empty, not just in the belly, but in the heart. Had he thrown up his spirit as well?

Do I even have a spirit? he thought.

Too many things cruxed him. The town's madness, of course; and the voice—most certainly. Hearing voices in one's head was not generally an indication of well being. What cruxed him most of all, though, was simply his own being here. Why had he come? For the truth, for shards of human realities to nourish his writing, but now he wondered. It made no sense, yet somehow he felt the opposite: that actually a *lack* of truth had evoked him. Vacuities, not realities. Wastelands.

Lies.

Absurdly, he sat beside the puddle of vomit, to reflect. Was throwing up catalytic to subjective conjecture? He felt rejected, but by what? By the mainstream? By society? In a sense he was—all writers were, and perhaps it was the backwash of his rejection that had instigated the summons, chosen him somehow. *Human truth is my sustenance. How powerful is the power of truth?* But the more he plied the speculation, the harder he laughed. The quest had backfired, leaving him to sit gutterside as his vomit spread into strange shapes between his feet. *Seeker, my ass,* he concluded. *Bugger truth.* All he cared about now was the next bus.

"Mother!" he heard.

The plea had sounded impoverished, a desperate whine like a lost child's.

Then: I SHOW YOU TRUTHS, SEEKER. SEEK. SEEK OUT THE SUSTENANCE OF TRUTH. SHOW ME YOUR WORTH.

The writer smirked. *What else have I got to do?* He could feel the churchfront as he approached, as one might sense a particular face in a crowd. Candlelight caused the nave's darkness to fitfully shift, populating the pews with a congregation of shadows, worshippers bereft of substance.

"Mother! I'm here!"

Aw, God, the writer thought, and it was the palest of thoughts, the bleakest and least sapient. What he saw numbed everything that he was. He stared toward the chancel as if encased in cement.

The coffin stood empty. Its previous tenant—the dead old woman—had been stripped of her last garments and lay stiff across the carpet, all gray-white dried skin and wrinkles, and a face like a dried fruit. Between the corpse's legs lay the priest, black trousers at his ankles, copulating furiously.

"I'll bring you back!" he promised, panting. His eyes squeezed shut in the most devout concentration. Sagging bags for breasts jiggled at the corpse's armpits.

"You're having sex with a corpse, for God's sake!" shouted the writer.

The fornication ceased. The rage of this ultimate coitus interruptus focused in the priest's eyes as sharply as cracked glass. "What?" he shouted.

"You're fucking your *mother's corpse!*"

"So?"

The writer shivered. "Correct me if I'm wrong—I'm not an expert on modern clergical protocol—but it's my understanding that priests aren't supposed to have sex, especially with their mothers, and more especially when their mothers are DEAD!"

The priest faltered, not at the writer's objection, but at some inner query. A sad recognition touched his face as he withdrew and straddled the embalmed cadaver. "I can't bring her back," he lamented. "No, not like this." His erection pulsed upward, a parodical stiff root. Forlornly, he picked something up.

The writer's guts shimmied. What the priest had picked up was a pair of heavy-duty roofing shears.

"There's only one way, I'm afraid," mourned the priest. The writer shouted "No no no! Holy shit! Don't do th—"

—as the priest unhesitantly clipped off his glans with the shears.

The obligatory scream shot about the nave; the glans fell to the carpet like a gumdrop.

The writer was backing away, his ears ringing. *I do not need to see this,* he thought. But something forced him to look, and by now he had a pretty good idea what that something was.

Blood jetted freely from the priest's clipped member— yes, freely as water out of a garden hose. "Mother, oh, Mother," he muttered, shuddering as the blood poured forth.

TRUTH, banged the voice in the writer's head as he plodded in shock back out onto the street. *Something's made everyone in this town crazy,* he realized.

NOT CRAZY. BLOOMED IN TRUTH, THE *REAL* TRUTH.

He ignored this; he had to. *So how come I'm not crazy?*

YOU'RE THE SEEKER, came his answer.

He gazed emptily down the street. He didn't feel crazy, he felt fine. So why was he hearing voices?

AH, YES, he heard. SUSTENANCE!

Was it really madness, or was it susceptibility, as the

voice seemed to infer? All his deliberating over truth, and what truth really was, had skirted one very important consideration. Perhaps truth was mutable. Like philosophy, art, technology—like life itself—perhaps old truths died and were replaced by new ones.

So the truth had changed? Was that it?

The writer banged through the swingdoors of the Crossroads.

"Look, he's back!" said the fat blonde. "It's the writer!"

"The *seeker*," corrected the keep. "Ready for a shooter?"

"Cram your shooters, rube, and you," he pointed violently at the fat blonde, "Stay the hell away from me." She burped in reply, halfway done with her next pizza. The redhead was still at the rail too; on a bar napkin she absently doodled stick figures with inordinately large genitals.

"What brings ya back?" asked the keep.

The fat blonde ripped off another belch, which sounded like a tree cracking. "Maybe he wants more pizza."

"You haven't seen my hopelessly inadequate boyfriend wandering around, have you?" the redhead asked.

Jesus, thought the writer. "All I want to know is when the next goddamn bus comes into this goddamn town."

"Call Trailways," invited the keep. "Pay phone's by the john."

Finally, a phone!

"But hold up a sec." The keep slapped a yellow shooter down. "Drink up, seeker. And don't worry, it's a—"

"I know, a tin roof." *Can't hurt, can it?* The writer shot the shooter back, froze mid-swallow, then spat it out. "What the fuck was that!"

"A Piss Shooter, partner." The keep's fly was open. "The house special. Bit more tasty than the last one, huh?"

"You're all a bunch of psychopaths!" screamed the writer.

"Crank up one of them Snot Shooters," suggested the fat blonde.

"Good thing I've had a cold all week. Makes 'em thicker, meatier." The keep applied an index finger to his left nostril, then loudly emptied his right one into a shooter glass. "Yeah, there's a beaut. Go for it, seeker."

The writer's head was reeling. "No, thanks. I'm trying to cut down."

"Cheers," said the fat blonde. She tossed it back neat, swallowing it more or less as a single lump. "Nice and thick!"

It just never ends, does it? The writer wobbled back to the pay phone, dropped in some change, and waited.

No dialtone.

"Goddamn this fuckin' shit-house piece of shit crazy-ass motherfuckin' town!" the writer articulated to the very best of his refined and erudite vocabulary. "Suckin' fuckin' redneck shitpile town ain't even got a fuckin' *phone* that works!"

"Phones haven't worked since last night," he was informed. It was the guy in the white shirt, who'd just come in the back way. He was hefting a shiny 44-oz aluminum softball bat. "Shh," he said next. "I want to surprise her." He snuck up behind the redhead, assumed a formidable batter's stance, and swung—

Ka-CRACK!

The impact of the bat to the redhead's right ear sent a big spurt of blood from her left. She flew off the stool like a golf ball off a tee and landed on the floor.

"How about *that?*" White Shirt softly inquired. "I'll bet *that* was big enough for you." The keep and fat blonde applauded. The writer just stared. White Shirt dragged the redhead out the back door by the throat.

"Still ain't found what'cha seek, huh, seeker?" commented the keep. "Still ain't found the truth. Well lemme tell ya somethin'. Truth can change."

The writer peered at him.

"I know what the truth is," claimed the fat blonde.

"Yeah?" the writer challenged. "Tell me then, you fat hunk of shit redneck walking trailer-park puke-machine. What is the truth?"

"It's black!"

Great. The truth is black. Wonderful. The writer started for the back door, but the keep implored, "Don't go yet. You'll miss my next one." He was lowering his trousers.

"Jizz Shooters!" cried the fat blonde.

Laughter followed the writer out the door. It made him feel rooked. Perhaps in their madness they knew something he didn't. Perhaps madness, in this case, was knowledge.

In the alley, White Shirt was eviscerating the redhead with a large hunting knife. Less than patiently, he rummaged through wet organs like someone looking for something, cufflinks maybe. "Give it back!" he shouted at the cooling gore. "I want it back!"

The writer leaned against the wall and lit a cigarette. "Buddy," he asked quietly. "Could you please tell me when the next bus comes through town?"

"There aren't any busses anymore. Things have changed."

Changed, the writer thought.

THE TRUTH HAS CHANGED, elaborated the voice. YOU WERE RIGHT. IT HAS BEEN REBORN, THROUGH *ME*. I LIVE ON IT.

The writer gave this some thought.

"I'm looking for my love," White Shirt remarked and gestured the redhead's opened belly. "I gave her my love, and I want it back." He scratched his head. "It's got to be in there somewhere."

"Love is in the heart," the writer pointed out.

"Yeah, but this girl was heartless."

"Well, the patriarchal Japanese used to believe that

love was in the belly, the intestines. They believed that the belly was the temple of the soul on earth. That's why they practiced ritual suicide by disembowelment—to release the soul and free the spiritual substantate of their love."

"Intestines," White Shirt contemplated. "So . . . if I gave *my* love to *her* . . ." He stared into the tilled gut, fingering its wares. "To get it back, I have to bring it into me?"

The writer shrugged. "I can't advise you. The decision is yours."

White Shirt began to eat the girl's intestines.

The writer's sweat surged. The redhead was as dead as dead could be, if not deader. Nevertheless, as her ex-lover steadily consumed the loops of her innards, her eyes snapped open and her head turned.

She looked directly at the writer.

"He's taking his love back," she giggled.

"I know," said the writer.

"It . . . tickles."

"I would imagine so."

The moon shone in each of her eyes as a perfect white dot. "Real truth sustains us, just in different ways."

Sustains, considered the writer. *Sustenance.*

"The end of your quest is waiting for you."

The writer gulped. "Tell me," he pleaded. "It's very important to me. *Please.*"

"Look for something black," she said, and died again.

The writer leapt the alley fence. The fat blonde had said the same thing. Black. But it was nighttime. How could he hope to find something black at night?

Then he heard something—a stout, distant *chugging.*

A motor, he realized.

Then he saw . . . what?

A glow?

A patch of light that was somehow, impossibly, black.

He was standing in a schoolyard—ironically a place of learning. The light shimmered in a rough trench-like bomb crater. *It's black,* he thought. In the distance sat the source of the motor noise: a squat U.S. Army armored personnel carrier.

The writer looked into the dropped back hatch.

"Don't go out there," warned a crisp yet muffled voice.

Murky red light bathed the inner compartment like blood in a lighted pool. A sergeant in a gas mask and full decontamination gear slouched at a console of radio equipment. Very promptly, he pointed a 9mm pistol at the writer's face.

The writer urinated in his pants, just as promptly. "Don't shoot me. I'm only a novelist."

The masked sergeant seemed very sad. "Bock and Jones. I had to send them out. It's a DECON field order. The lowest ranking men go into the final exclusion perimeter first."

Final exclusion perimeter?

"I think it got them," the sergeant said

It, the writer reckoned.

In the mask's portals, the sergeant's eyes looked insane. "When my daughter was an infant, I'd rock her in my lap every night."

"That's, uh, that's nice, sergeant."

"It gave me a hard on . . . She's fourteen now. I drilled a hole in the bathroom wall so I can watch her take showers."

"They have counselors for things like that, I think."

A dark suboctave suffused into the words. "At midnight, the wolf howls."

The writer winced. "What?"

"I never knew my father."

Then the sergeant shot himself in the head.

Sound and concussion hit the writer like a physical weight. *BANG!* It shoved him out of the rumbling vehicle as the sergeant's mask quickly filled up with blood.

I HUNGER FOR TRUTH TOO, loomed the voice. BUT TO SEE IT, IT MUST BE REVEALED. DO YOU UNDERSTAND? YOU *MUST* UNDERSTAND.

The writer strayed into the yard. Yes, he thought he *did* understand now. Here was what his whole life had been leading him to. All that he'd sought, in his absurd pretensions as a *seeker,* had brought him to this final test. There could be no going back. His preceptor awaited, the *ultimate* seeker.

A second decon soldier lay dead in the grass. There were no hands at the ends of his arms, and the stumps appeared burned. Some colossal inner pressure had forced his brains out his ears.

"Get out of here, you civvie fucker!" someone commanded. A third soldier strode through shadows, a kid no more than twenty. "The light! It's mine!"

"Are you quite sure about that?"

"It's . . . God. I'm taking it!"

A TEST? WATCH.

"Watch!" the boy cried. "I'll prove it's mine!" He ran manic to the trench, his young face in awe above the radiant black blur. "Hard-fucking-core, man! I'm taking *God!*" He put his hands into the light, eyes wide as moons, and picked it up. But in only a second the light fell back to its resting place, melting through the boy's hands. He stood up stiff and convulsed, a silent scream in his lips.

The voice trumpeted. ALAS. FAILURE.

This disconcerted the writer, for he knew he was next. For the last time in his life, then, he asked himself the ever important query. *How powerful is the power of truth?*

I'LL SHOW YOU.

The boy's innards prolapsed through his mouth in a few slow, even pulses; the writer thought of a fat snake squeezing from its hole. Lungs, liver, heart, g.i. tract—everything that was inside now hung heavily outside, glimmering. Then the red heart, amid it all, stopped beating, and the boy fell dead.

ONLY FAITH CAN SAVE YOU NOW.

"I kind of figured that," the writer admitted.

THE TRUTH IS MY SUSTENANCE. I EXIST TO EXPOSE IT, TO GIVE IT FLESH. I DRAW IT OUT SO THAT IT CAN BE REAL AND, HENCE, SUSTAINING. DO YOU UNDERSTAND? TOO OFTEN THE TRUTH HIDES UNDERNEATH. WITHOUT REVELATION, WHAT PURPOSE CAN THERE BE IN TRUTH?

Good point, the writer mused.

WE'RE BOTH SEEKERS, WE BOTH HAVE QUESTS. LET OUR QUESTS JOIN HANDS NOW IN THE REAL LIGHT OF WHAT WE SEEK.

"Yes," said the writer.

WILL YOU MINISTER TO ME?

"Yes."

THEN THERE IS BUT ONE DOOR LEFT FOR YOU TO ENTER. GLORY OR FAILURE. TRUTH OR LIES. THE TEST OF *YOUR* FAITH IS UPON YOU.

The writer looked into the shimmering trench. This would either be the end or the beginning; it was providence. To turn away now would reduce his entire life to a lie. He began to reach down, softly smiling.

I am the seeker, he thought.

He put his hands into the light.

YES!

He picked it up. He looked at it, cradled it. The glory on his face felt brighter than a thousand suns. The test was done, and he had passed.

Was the black light weeping?

CARRY ME AWAY, it said.

He took it into the Army vehicle and closed the back hatch.

THERE'S SO MUCH, SO MUCH FOR US TO SEEK.

In the driver's compartment, the writer lit a cigarette. *Looks simple enough,* he observed. A t-bar, an accelerator, and a brake. Automatic transaxle, low and second. The fuel gauge read well over half.

He thought of sustenance, the first pronouncement of the light. This town had been too small; that was the problem: tiny, dry. There weren't enough people here to provide the truth its proper flesh. But that was all right. He knew it wouldn't take long to get to a really big city.

SUSTENANCE, SEEKER, whispered the light like a lover.

The seeker put the vehicle into gear and began to drive.

PLEASE LET ME OUT

"What's a woman to do?" Dee posed the question past her Packard-Bell computer. Her bleached-blond hair looked like bright straw. "Liars, cheaters—all of them. I've never in my life dated a guy who didn't run around behind my back."

Marianne, the redhead with a face reminiscent of a pugnosed Meryl Streep, lamented in agreement. "Goddamn men, they got their brains in their pants. I mean, I never cheated on Willy, and let me tell you, I had plenty of opportunities. I gave that bastard my heart and soul, and next thing I know he's playing musical beds with half the barmaid staff."

Joyce Lipnick couldn't help but overhear these vocal ruminations: the CSS bug in Dee's intercom speaker was Joyce's ear to the outer office. She didn't consider this eavesdropping; she was just being careful. When you were a managing partner at the number-three law firm in the country, you *had* to be careful.

But the girls (Dee, her paralegal; and Marianne, the floor receptionist) were right. *What's a woman to do?* Joyce reflected in the plush, cherry-paneled office. Czanek, the sleazy P.I. she'd hired, had proved Scott's rampant infidelities. With full-color glossies, no less. How could Joyce ever erase those images? Scott, the love of her life, servicing his secret bevy via every conceivable sexual position. He left her no choice.

"I couldn't believe it," Marianne rambled. "I came home early one day, and there's Willy with that hussie from the first floor, and he's going at it like a lapdog."

Like a lapdog, Joyce pondered. Has Scott performed likewise? Czanek had verified at least five "steadies," but suspected four more. "Your man gets around, Ms. Lipnick, a real nutchase," he'd eloquented upon receipt of his $200-per-day fee. "Of course, a good-looking boy like that, it stands to reason."

Stands to reason. Joyce could've spit. *I give him a car, a beautiful home, money, credit cards, not to mention all my love, and he repays me by sewing his oats with a bunch of bimbos!*

"Yeah, you tell me," Dee reiterated over the hidden bug. "What's a woman to do?"

Joyce sympathized . . . But she herself had *done* something. She pressed her intercom. "Dee, I forgot to tell you. File a health insurance termination for Scott. Right away."

The pause yawned over the speaker. "A termination, Ms. Lipnick? But I thought Scott was on vacation."

"No, Dee. He was fired. What good is a copy boy who's late every other day? And I want those deposition digests for the Air National case on my desk in an hour. I'll look pretty idiotic if I can't go into court and cross examine those grapeheads on prior testimony. Oh, and remember, we only have a week to get out the preliminary jury instructions for the JAX Avionics appeal."

"Yes, Ms. Lipnick."

Joyce switched off and listened to the bug.

"Did you hear that shit?" Dee whispered to Marianne. "She fired Scott!"

"And he was so cute," Marianne lamented. "That face, and—Christ, did he have a body."

"Tell me about it." Dee's whisper lowered. "That guy could go all night. It was unreal."

"Dee! You mean you . . . With *Scott?*"

"A bunch of times," she giggled. "Let's just say that all my sick leave's used up for the year, and there're a lot of worn out beds at the Regency Inn."

"Dee!"

But even this news didn't dishearten Joyce. Not now. Not ever again, she resolved. *What's a woman to do, girls? I wish I could tell you, because I did it.*

And as for Dee . . . *Giddy little slut.* Joyce would trump something and fire her next week.

"Darling?" Joyce set down her litigation bag and unlocked the steel-framed bedroom door. She supposed it was fitting: that Scott's prison be a bedroom. Poetic justice with a twist.

He was waiting for her in bed. "God, honey, I missed you." His strong arms reached out for her. *He's just so sweet,* she thought. *How can I be mad at him?* She decided not to even bring up the business with Dee. That was over now. All of his infidelities were over. Instead, she kicked off her shoes, climbed into the luxurious four-poster, and was embraced by him at once. "I missed you more," she whispered.

"Uh-uh." His kiss devoured her: it took all the stresses of the day and banished them. It made her forget everything. In just seconds, she was so *hot.* His tongue roved her mouth. His hands—strong, assured, insistent—shucked her right out of the charcoal cardigan, then stripped off her white Evan-Picone silk blouse. Nimble fingers released her breasts from lace bra and stroked her nipples. *Oh God, oh my love,* came the helpless thought. His mouth sucked her breath out of her chest.

"Baby," he murmured. "Please."

Her own kisses descended then. Scott's hands peeled away her skirt as Joyce played her tongue over his nipples, then licked ever downward. "Sweetheart . . ." His fingers finnicked in her coiffed black hair, pushing. "Do you love me?" she asked and admitted his penis into her mouth before he could answer. He squirmed, moaning. She sucked slow and hard while her fingers explored testicles that felt large and heavy as hen's eggs. "Do you love me?" Again. "Do you love me, darling?" Again, again. "Yes," he panted. Her tongue traced around the gorged dome, teasing the tiny egress. This only heightened his squirming, as Joyce squirmed herself to get shed of her panties.

"Joyce—honey . . . I love you *so* much."

"Do you? Do you really?"

"Yes!"

"Then show me." She crawled up to poise herself, then placed her sex right onto his mouth. Her eyes rolled back at the instant flood of sensation.

"You taste lovely," he murmured.

Later—many, many hours later—Joyce lay sated and deliciously sore. She sipped Perrier-Jouet and watched him sleep. So beautiful, so loving. Czanek's photographs reared in her mind. And Dee? *Don't think about it. The little tramp.* Joyce could scream thinking of Scott with someone else. Those strong hands, the broad sculpted chest, shoulders, and back, and that gorgeous curved cock. *With someone else?* she pondered. *No, never again.*

Who could provide for him better than Joyce? Four hundred thousand a year, a spacious house on the water, and anything else he'd ever need. *And love,* she thought. *Real, mature, guiding love.*

She'd never been with a man like him: so passionate, so deft.

His ability to sense her—her moods, her needs, her desires—was nearly psychic, and the orgasms he gave her—a dozen hot thrumming gifts each night—wrung pleasure from

31

her nerves like warm water being twisted from a sponge. Often he'd make love to her til she simply couldn't move.

And he would understand the rest, in time. When he was older and realized that Joyce knew what was best for him. That's all that mattered. *The truth,* she thought.

Later, his whispers woke her. "Darling?" His hands traced her warm flesh. "Darling?" He nuzzled her breasts, stroked her back and buttocks. "Once more," he whispered.

Joyce's heart pattered against her fatigue. "I don't think I can do it again, honey. You wear me out!"

"Yes," he insisted. "Yes." He rolled over on top of her, pinned her arms above her head as his erection slid directly into her sex. "I love to make you come." The deep, gentle strokes, like a lovely derrick of flesh, drew expertly in and out of her. Joyce felt electrified. Her breasts filled, her nipples distended to pebbles. Oh, she could do it again, all right. Always. Always. Her hands plied his muscled buttocks as he rocked into her, and his penis—always so hard for her, so large and knowing—tilled her salt-damp depths without abatement. Orgasms like sweet dreams unloosed in her, strings of them, carrying her away with their succulent spasms. *I'm in heaven,* she affirmed. *I'm in heaven every night.*

When he'd finished, Joyce lay immobile, shellacked in sweat and afterglow. His semen ran out of her, so much of it. Scott coddled her, soothing her inflamed breasts, kissing up and down her throat. "Joyce, I know I was bad before," he whispered.

No, she thought. *Please.*

"But I really do love you. I would never want anyone else again, ever. Please believe me, darling . . ."

Please don't . . .

"But it drives me crazy, sitting here by myself all day waiting for you. Each hour you're gone feels like a week."

Joyce was wilting.

"Oh, please, honey. Please let me out."

She stroked his hair, touched the side of his handsome face. "I will," she promised. "I will."

But the promise, like many made among lovers, was a lie. She knew she could never, ever let him out.

Their morning ritual: breakfast in bed. Nude, they fed each other languidly—Eggs Benedict, Iranian caviar on toast points, chickoried coffee—as their bodies pressed. Then she showered and began to dress. She always dressed slowly, knowing his fascination for watching her. It made her feel sexy, delightfully lewd.

"You're so beautiful," he said. His clear baby-blue eyes fixed on her from the bed, "I might have to touch myself."

"Don't you dare," Joyce said behind a sly grin. Of course he touched himself; all men did. But did he think about her when he did it? Facing him, she snapped her bra, then teasingly drew her stockings up her legs. "I want you to save it for me, all of it. Every drop."

"Well . . ." His grin cut into her. "I'll try."

She fastened her floral waist-skirt, then buttoned up the placketed Jacquard top.

"Give me something," he said.

"What?"

"Give me your panties."

Joyce blushed. "Scott, I can't go to work without—"

"Yes you can. I want them with me, so I can think about you sitting there at the office with nothing underneath. I'll think about your beautiful pussy all day, and how bad I want to taste it."

God! Joyce's blush deepened. When he talked dirty like that, she was helpless. She slipped off her panties and tossed them to Scott, who plucked them out of the air and held them fast to his chest.

"I love you," he said.

"Not as much as I love you," she assured him, and then she assured him even further when she left the bedroom and locked the heavy hardwood door behind her.

It was for his own good, anyway. Cruel, yes. Extreme, certainly.

But left to his own devices, Scott would cheat on any woman he became involved with. *What kind of life is that?* Joyce inquired. *What would he become?* All Scott had were his looks. Little education, and less drive. Without Joyce's guidance, he'd be a drifter all his life. *I'm saving him from himself. He'll thank me someday.*

Joyce idled the Porsche into the firm's underground lot, then strode, Bali heels clicking, to the elevator. *Of course, keeping a man locked in your bedroom presents some legal problems.* But why worry? The windows were Lexan set into steel frames, the doors were all locked, and the great waterfront house stood so remote he could yell till his face turned blue and no one would hear him.

"Good morning, Ms. Lipnick," Dee and Marianne greeted in unison when Joyce entered the front office.

"Good morning, girls." She repressed the urge to frown at Dee, whose large breasts threatened to erupt from her blouse. *If she ever has a child,* Joyce postulated, *it'll overdose on milk.* "Don't forget those Delany 'rogs, Dee. I want them out today."

"Yes, Ms. Lipnick."

"And those JAX instructions—today."

"Yes, Ms. Lipnick."

Blond ditz. Thinks she can steal away any man with those big boobs. In her office, Joyce contemplated her own breasts in the mirror. They looked fine now—the $5,500 implant job had taken care of the sag. And as for her dreaded cellulite, good old Dr. Liposuction had made short work of it. Scott being so handsome, Joyce felt the maintenance of her own appearance was an obligation. *You're fifty-one now, Joyce, and you're not getting any younger.* Soon would be time for another lift, or a chemical peel. Thank God for plastic surgeons.

But the two fresh young girls outside inhibited her. She pressed her intercom. "Marianne, come into my office please."

"Yes, Ms. Lipnick?" said the receptionist a moment later.

"Come in please, and close the door." Joyce stood up, mildly befuddled. "This may sound silly, Marianne, but I'd like your opinion about something. Your honest opinion."

"Sure."

"Am I . . ." The question drifted. "Do you think . . ."

"What is it, Ms. Lipnick?"

"What I mean is, do you think I'm pretty?"

The young receptionist fidgeted at the question, "Well, of course, Ms. Lipnick. You're a very attractive woman. In fact, I heard some the associates talking the other day, and they were saying how they couldn't understand why a woman so attractive wasn't married."

Joyce brimmed. "Ah, well. Thank you, Marianne. It's very nice that you related that to me. But please don't tell anyone I asked."

"Of course not, Ms. Lipnick."

Marianne left. Joyce reseated herself and thought, *There, see? Nothing to be paranoid about . . .* Nevertheless, she turned on the bug.

"Dee! You'll never guess what the Ice-Bitch just asked."

Joyce's jaw set. *Oh, so it's the Ice-Bitch is it?* "She asked me if I thought she was *pretty!*"

Dee chirped laughter. "What did you say?"

"I'm not stupid, I told her she was very attractive."

35

Marianne chirped a bit of her own laughter. "I even made up a lie about how the associates thought so too."

"I still can't get over that boob-job she got. Thinks no one noticed. One day they're like pancakes hanging to her waist, and the next day she's Dolly Parton."

"What an old bag!" Dee whispered.

An old bag, huh? Joyce smirked back her ire. Pancakes. She'd trump something up on Marianne and fire her next week, too. Then the two little airheads could stand in the unemployment line together. See if their youth put food on the table. See if their big tits paid the rent.

That night Scott spread Joyce Lipnick out like a feast. A feast of passion. A feast of warm flesh. Her orgasms rushed out of her, each a torrid spirit unleashed by her lover's ministrations. It was like this every night now: any pleasure Joyce could imagine was made manifest in the locked room's gossamer dark.

Via mouth, hand, or genitals, Scott left no orifice untended, no anticipation unslaked. Time passed not in minutes, nor hours, but in the repeated pulses of her bliss. His love consumed her, it carried her away on angels' wings to a demesne of passion and indefectibility that was theirs and theirs alone.

It would be like this, she knew, for the rest of their lives. Till death do them part. Scott's imprisonment was really his salvation, his *freedom* to love and to be loved to the ultimate limit of truth. What could be more wonderful, or more real, than that?

Later, they embraced, laved in sweat, lacquered in joy. Joyce fell asleep, content by the feel of his copious semen in her sex, and the trail of its aftertaste glowing down her throat. But she also fell asleep to his whispers, and the night's ever-faint plea:

"Please, Joyce. Please let me out."

36

***

Weekends unfolded in sheer hedonism. Rich meals in bed, between frenetic bouts of love. Once Scott ate Steak Tartar out of the cleft of Joyce's bosom. Another time he'd poured an entire bottle of Martell Cordon Bleu over her body and licked it off. Salmon roe was daintily eaten off of genitalia. Sashimi was lain out on abdomens. Once Scott had even filled her sex with baby Westcott oysters—flown in fresh from Washington–and plucked each one out with his tongue.

Was this so bad, so cruel, to share with him life's delicacies? To enjoy each other in unbridled abandon? What difference did it make that the door was locked? Between hard and heavy love-making, they'd loll in the jacuzzi, sipping champagne from Cristal d'Arques flutes. Swirls of warm bubbles cosseted them. Joyce couldn't resist; any proximity to Scott lit a lewd fuse in her that never went out. Frequently she'd fellate him beneath the water, gentling stroking his buttock's groove. Scott shuddered amid the luxurious swirls, then Joyce would coax out his climax with her hand and watch the precious curls of sperm churn away in the foam . . .

Week mornings shared the same feasts of the palate. "I've got to keep my baby well-fed," she'd say. "You'll need the energy tonight." Then he'd watch her shower and dress—in total adoration. Giving him these images of herself kept her aroused all day. To hell with what those silly tramps thought. If Joyce wasn't really beautiful, then why was Scott always so hot for her? Sometimes she'd make love to him just before leaving: fully dressed but for panties she'd straddle him amid the covers, and just ride him until his climax answered the demand of her loins. Or she'd service him orally, and swallow up his seed. "That should tide you over till I come home, hmm?"

This particular morning, though, he repeated his former request just as she would leave. *My darling fetishist,* she thought.

"Give me something," he said.

"Hmmm?" Joyce coyly replied.

"Your bra," he decided. "Give me your bra."

"Oh, so it's my bra this time?"

"That's right. Take it of right now and give it to me." His smile teased at her, his awesome pectorals flexed as he lay with his fingers laced behind his head. "So I can think about you sitting at your desk all day long with your bare breasts rubbing against your blouse. I'll think about your beautiful nipples getting hard, tingling. I'll think about kissing them, licking them . . . all day . . ."

Joyce's face flushed. She'd get excited just listening to him! She removed her blouse, tossed him the sheer, lacy bra, and redressed.

Scott held the bra like an icon. "I love you," he affirmed.

"I love you too, and I'll show you how much when I come home."

And when she left, and locked the sturdy door behind her, Scott's eyes squeezed shut so hard that tears leaked out. His hands mangled the bra, twisting, twisting, as though it were not a bra at all, but a garrote.

Joyce's guilt frequently presented itself by midday. So she did what all good lawyers did with guilt: she rationalized it out of existence. *Look at what I'm absolving him from,* she attested. Shallow interludes, bogus relationships, disease. What she'd done was actually an act of love—a superlative one—and she knew that already he was beginning to realize that. Her mere sleeping with him was proof, wasn't it? At night Joyce locked herself in with him. She was open to him, vulnerable; in a sense, she was at his mercy every night. Scott easily had the physical capability to kill her if he wanted to. But not once had he even threatened violence.

Because he loves me, she realized, braless and musing at her desk. *Because he's finally beginning to understand. Without me, he knows he's powerless against the seductions of the world. If I hadn't taken the necessary steps, he'd still be out there cheating on me, wasting his life and disillusioning himself. Causing pregnancies. Catching chlamydia, herpes, AIDS.*

He knows now. This is the only way.

Between deposition rewrites, Joyce turned on her bug. Dee and Marianne, the magpies, chattered away as always.

"Gary was such a dream. I mean, we were perfect together."

"Dee, Gary was a conniving, treacherous *cockhound.* He was putting the make on your mother, for God's sake."

"Yeah, and both my sisters, too. I hate to think how many women he went to bed with while we were engaged."

"They take everything for granted. The minute they find a good thing, they're snuffling around every skirt in sight."

"Men. Sometimes you could just lock them up."

Joyce nodded a curt approval. *Ladies and gentlemen of the court, the verdict is in, and the judgment in unanimous.*

She thought about Scott all day, her tingling nipples an interminable reminder of her bralessness. She imagined Scott's adroit tongue gingerly encircling the tender areolae, his heavenly mouth sucking them out. She imagined his hands describing the contours of her breasts—adoring them, worshiping them. And she imagined much more, till the urge to masturbate overwhelmed her. *No!* she demanded. *Wait.* Why touch herself when in just a few hours *he* would be touching her?

Marianne buzzed. "Ms. Lipnick? There's a man to see you . . ."

A man? Probably some counter-lit bozo from the JAX Avionics appeal. *Wants to settle now for five or ten mil. Don't hold your breath, pal.* "Send him in, please," she said.

Past the threshold stepped a tall, well-postured man in a fine pinstripe suit. Short sandy hair, blue eyes. *Handsome,* she thought. But something bland like a stoic chill set into his face. "Ms. Joyce Lipnick?" he queried. "My name is Spence."

Joyce stood up, hard-pressed not to frown. "Well, what can I do for you . . . Spence?"

"Oh, I'm sorry. I should say *Lieutenant* Spence."

Lieutenant?

" . . . District Major Case Section."

Joyce felt forged in ice—

Spence continued, "You are under arrest, Ms. Lipnick, for first-degree sexual misconduct, abduction, and sexual imprisonment, and those are just the trifling charges."

"Now see here, Lieutenant!" Joyce erupted. "What in God's name are you talking about?"

Behind the policeman, Dee and Marianne could be seen peaking in, their faces pinched, inquisitive. Spence looked like a well-dressed golem as he paused to assay Joyce's expression.

And then it dawned on her. *God, no. Somehow Scott got—*

"He got out, Ms. Lipnick," Spence informed her. "It must've taken him hours to pick the lock on the door—he did it with two bent bra-clips. Then he got to the phone and called us."

Joyce's nipples instantly lost their arousal. She could only stand there now, opposing this brazen cop as she felt all the blood run out of her face. "I—" she attempted. But the words dissolved. In fact, her entire being felt as though it were dissolving right there before the witness of the whole world. Eventually she was able to croak, "I had no choice. He was cheating on me."

"Well, you certainly took care of that inconvenience." Spence, for only a moment, spared a smile. "And it gives me great pleasure, Ms. Lipnick, to inform you that you have the right to remain silent, and that anything you say . . ."

Joyce paid no attention to the rest of the policeman's obligatory mirandization. Instead, paling, she thought in scorn, *The goddamn ungrateful bastard got out. I should've known he'd try something like this. How could I be so stupid?*

And what was that Spence had initially said?

—and those are just the trifling charges—

Spence, at least, had a lawyer's wit.

Dee and Marianne looked on, aghast. Joyce's face felt like pallid wax as Spence handcuffed her. "Don't you have anything to say, Ms. Lipnick?" the policeman inquired. "In my experience, criminals generally have a comment or two upon arrest."

"I think I will observe my right to remain silent," Joyce blandly replied.

"A commendable decision."

But as Joyce was ushered out, she couldn't escape the inscrutable image—Scott, travailing down the hall for the phone. Nor the final consideration: *I guess I should have cut his arms off too,* she thought.

THE ORDER OF NATURE

D.C. was only twenty miles away; Haggert was pretty sure he could make it, and he didn't mind the temporary delay, even in spite of its rather grueling cause: the car wreck on State Route 50. He guessed it would take an hour or so for the police and EMTs to clear the road of its wreckage and bodies, and he didn't want to sit out here for the whole time. *I think a detour is in order,* he thought. He edged his Lincoln Town Car over onto the shoulder.

Blood blared on the asphalt; the wind-chill was ten degrees, and it made the blood freeze, a sheen more black than red as the police lit ranks of road flares. Suddenly the night was hissing. One woman's head, severed via the action of being catapulted through the windshield of her Subaru, had landed perfectly right side up, resting on its stump, at the shoulder before the exit ramp. Haggert squeezed the Lincoln by, and the woman's head, eyes still miraculously open, seemed to appraise him as he passed. He even thought she was smiling.

Careful, careful. He didn't want to clip the fender of the vehicle in front of him; it would be a tight fit. He was a cautious driver. When he squeezed by he thought, *Thank God.* He was cautious, yes, but not patient. He didn't want to sit in a line of motionless traffic—that would make him feel futile and vulnerable—so he turned off onto the main road into downtown Annapolis. *Just find a little bar or café, wait an hour, and then get back on the highway.* The evening felt muffled, from the cold. Not many cars out downtown, which suited him fine, but lots of shoppers on the sidewalk, huddled with scarves and hats and big smiles and packages under their arms. Christmas lights glittered along the storefronts of West Street, and he could hear music and chimes. It reminded him of the season, but that notion, a moment later, made him feel dry inside. Holiday good cheer? Good will toward your fellow man? No, it was all manufactured, all commercial—an instigation to urge people to spend money. Greed and materialism were becoming part of the natural order, it seemed. *There's no real good will any more,* he thought, squinting over the wheel. *Has there ever been?*

He idled past a wine bar, an Asian-fusion restaurant, a deli. UNDERCROFT, read a swing-sign. *Looks good to me.* An Irish Coffee would do the trick right now, to stave off the cold. He pulled the Lincoln into the side lot, jerked up his collar, but paused before cutting the ignition. The news flowing out of the radio cauterized him: DOW down third week straight, unemployment up, U.S. Air Force drops "daisy-cutter" munition by mistake on Red Cross relief warehouse, Chechnya rebels release homemade phosgene gas in Moscow subway, killing 160. Haggert shook his head, turned the motor off, and walked into the tavern. *No. No good will anywhere. Why bother looking?* He knew that now.

The Undercroft was an old Federal-Period tavern, still showing its original brick-and-mortar walls. Short steps took him down, and a brass bell chimed when he pushed through, shuddering relief at the heat. *Yes, an Irish Coffee is just what I need.* But when he stepped in, a weird stasis looked back at him. Only a handful of patrons were inside, all seated oddly around a big table before the fieldstone fireplace. Were they all friends? They looked too diverse.

No music, no talk, just a faint newscaster from a local news program on the high TV in the corner. No one moved.

What is this? Haggert thought.

Then there was a gun in his face.

Talk about terrific luck, he mused. *I came in here for an Irish Coffee and I get taken hostage instead.* There were seven of them: the Caucasian male with glasses and goatee, the Black Guy, the Jew, the Muslim, the Straw Blonde, the Brunette, and Haggert.

And an eighth: the Redneck with the Gun.

It was a big gun, a SIG-226 nine-millimeter. It dwarfed the Redneck's ruddy face, though the Redneck, too, was formidable. Stocky, hard in construction-work muscles, ponytail pulled back over the scuffed leather jacket and ZZ TOP t-shirt. *He's cracked,* Haggert saw at once, just by the eyes. They were raving.

Evidently, everyone in the tavern had been ordered to throw their wallets on the center table. The Redneck was looking through them, but his eyes kept flicking up, as he took the cash out and stuffed it in his pocket. "I'm not fucking around," he declared, though he clearly didn't need to. "This isn't just a robbery, it's a mass-murder. Any of you religious? Now's time to say your prayers."

Under his breath, the Caucasian muttered, "Fuck," then began to whisper some plea to God. The Muslim smiled, while the Jew looked more annoyed than scared.

"Just thought I'd give you the option," said the Redneck. He waved the gun, but there were several more stuffed in his belt. He locked the front door, flipped over the CLOSED sign. It was a good location for such a thing. A basement bar? Passersby probably wouldn't be able to hear gun fire.

"No one leaves here alive, except me," the Redneck said. "Just so you know. But we're gonna have some fun first."

Haggert had heard more encouraging things.

"Why are you doing this?" the Blonde peeped. She sat at the table next to Haggert. She was terribly pretty, the flaxen-blond hair shining shoulder-length, ocean-blue eyes, perfect bosom. She looked like something Peter Paul Rubens might paint were he alive today, a casual—even innocent—portrait in designer jeans and argent-white blouse. Drunkenness and terror, somehow, made her even more attractive. "We haven't done anything to you," she continued, almost stuttering.

The Redneck's eyes pinched up. "You remind me of my wife. That's not good."

"But-but-but," she began, and Haggert faintly shook his head at her, squeezed her hand under the table.

"We're all very scared," Haggert tried to break some ice. "But maybe we can help you. No one here means you any harm."

Redneck shoved the gun forward. "Buddy, everybody means me harm."

"We don't," Black Guy said. He looked like Arsenio Hall, only portly. "My guess is you've had some tough times. We all have."

To himself, Haggert agreed. It was easy to see, almost a cliche in this day and age. Someone else ruined by the holidays, pushed over the edge. *He doesn't care anymore.* That was the scariest part.

"We're all in this together, man," Black Guy added.

"Shut the fuck up," the Brunette muttered under her breath. She gnashed her teeth. She wasn't butch, just tough-looking, attractive but rough-edged, hard-eyed. "You're just gonna piss him off more."

Redneck laughed. "Hey, everybody pisses me off. The whole fuckin' world pisses me off. My wife divorced me for the neighbor, my kids hate me, I just got laid off at the site, and look—" His gun hand bid the door. "It's Christmas!"

Indeed. Through the door, the bar's Christmas lights twinkled, and on the television, Santa Claus ho-ho-ho'd through a commercial for an electric razor. The Redneck grinned at his gun: "Yeah, merry fuckin' Christmas."

It's a lost cause, Haggert realized at once. No "talking" would alter the situation. This guy was off the deep end.

The TV interrupted with grimness when the commercial was over: "Channel Eleven News has learned from anonymous but credible sources that radioactive waste is missing from the Calvert Cliffs Nuclear Power Plant, material that could potentially be used for a makeshift weapon known as a 'dirty nuke.' However, authorities at the plant assured us that this material is accounted for and that nothing hazardous could ever be stolen from the Calvert Cliffs plant. On a similar front, residents of Edgewood, Maryland, are complaining of a sixty-percent increase in obstructive respiratory disorders among local children under the age of ten, since rumors began three years ago of underground leaks at the nearby Edgewood Arsenal, one of the Army's largest depots of buried chemical weapons materials. Army authorities deny the allegations, citing that all such buried materials were destroyed in the late eighties as part of the Chemical Weapons Disarmament Treaty signed between the U.S. and Russia—"

The Redneck howled, "Yeah, right, and if you believe that, I got a fuckin' bridge I can sell ya."

The TV continued: "But that's just the local front. Three parishes in southern Louisiana are still being hit hard due to catastrophic lowland flooding after a week of torrential rain. Thirty-one people were killed today, eleven of them children, when a flash-flood caused by a levy break inundated the entire town of Amyville. Several hundred homes were completely destroyed, and police and local fire officials have verified that the levy break was caused by a dynamite detonation by an unknown perpetrator."

"See that, see that?" the Redneck goaded. He seemed enthused. "It's fuckin' Christmas and look what people are doing to each other. Stealing radioactive shit to make bombs, hiding nerve gas and shit, blowing up levies on purpose. The whole world is shit. There's nothing but hate. Well, lemme tell you something, I hate too."

More: ". . . and on the global front, Israeli security forces bombed a former PLO safehouse in the West Bank, citing a dozen casualties, after launching recon flights over Syria. Syria has recently been blasted by the Israeli Parliament for allegedly hiding weapons of mass-destruction secreted in from Iraq after Iraqi consent to UN weapons inspections . . ."

The Redneck raged: "See! See! Everybody wants to kill each other. Well, I wanna kill too. I'm gonna be like everybody else. Fuck it. I don't give a shit anymore. All these psychos out there, all these radicals and terrorists. They're doin' this to make a statement."

"Is that what you're doing?" the Jewish man asked. "Making a statement by killing a bunch of people you don't know?"

Silence slammed down like a guillotine. Haggert thought sure that the Jewish man had just spoken his last words.

Instead, the Redneck just said, "Yeah. This is my statement. I've got some shit to say back to the world. The world's fucked me over. Tonight I fuck back." He walked to the Muslim. "You. I want to know about you." He leaned closer. "Tell me something. What do you hate?"

"I hate all deliberate enemies of Islam," the man replied. "It's nothing that anyone here could really understand. You have to be there to see it."

"What about me?" the Redneck goaded. "I don't give a shit about Islam, but I'm pointing a fucking gun at you. Do you hate me?"

"No. I love you as I love any creation of God."

"Hey, if I'm a creation of God, then God's royally fucked up. If there's a God, then He's a prick for fucking up my life."

"I will pray for you," the Muslim said in a clipped accent, "that things will get better for you."

"Don't pray for me . . . Mahhad," the Redneck continued after he looked at the Muslim's ID in his wallet. "Pray for yourself," and—

BAM!

The Muslim's left eye seemed to vanish in its socket, then the man's body flew out of the chair and crumpled to the floor. Behind him a spout of blood and cranial matter hung off a painting of a ram like a great scarlet wing.

Everyone had jumped in their seat at the inordinately loud shot; Haggert's heart tripped. Gunsmoke creamed the Redneck's face and slowly dissipated around his mad smile.

"Shit," someone muttered.

"You didn't have to do that, man," the Caucasian said. He stood up but looked crestfallen, like he knew he was going to die soon and that no force on earth would alter that.

"Want me to do it again?" The Redneck pointed the pistol.

"Let me ask one favor," the Caucasian absurdly said. "Monday Night Football's on right now, the Redskins are playing the Giants. I need the Skins to win. Can I please change the channel, check the score? Then you can kill me."

"The man has his priorities," Haggert remarked, and several people actually laughed. The comment broke the terrifying stasis of murder's aftershock.

"Sure," the Redneck said.

CNN snapped over to football. The Caucasian stared raptly at the screen, as though football might save his immortal soul, that it might protect him. He watched, staring upward, as the last seconds of the game ran out, then he signed through an exhausted smile. His team had won. "I guess I can die now," he said.

"Oh, you'll die, but only when I say." The Redneck was eyeing an ID in another wallet, then approached the Jew. "I want to know more about *this* guy. Tell me . . . Sy. What do you think?"

The man looked up, testy but not quite defiant. "Think about what?"

"I just blew away an Islamic dude. He hates Jews, he thinks Israel doesn't have the right to exist. He's probably from Saudi fucking Arabia or some place where they secretly give money and explosives to the suicide bombers so they can kill your people. You must be pretty happy that I blew him away."

Sy paused. "I'm not happy. You want to know what I am?"

"What?"

"I'm disgusted."

Watch it, Haggert thought.

"Stand up."

Sy rose, rather shakily, but never taking his eyes off the Redneck. Now the Redneck had the Black's wallet. He took the money out of it, then examined the ID. "George? You too. Stand up, stand next to Sy, by the wall."

George did so, having to step over the Muslim's body.

The Redneck looked at a few more wallets, got a few more names. The Brunette froze when he pointed the gun at her from across the room and said, "Sharon, stand up, right where you are. Don't go over to the wall with Sy and George. Just stand up there."

Sharon came to her feet, trembling. The Redneck kept the gun on her, but pulled another pistol from his belt, a revolver, and threw it to her. Her hands were shaking but, miraculously, she caught it.

"There's one bullet in that gun, Sharon, just one. Now, I know you're not stupid enough to even *think* about pointing it at me. Right?"

"Right," she muttered.

"Pick the guy you're going to kill. Sy or George. You have to kill one of them. If you don't, I'll kill you. Do you believe me?"

Sharon nodded.

BAM!

She shot George without deliberation. She'd aimed for his head but the round went low and hit the man in the throat. He fell down, flailing in agony, gargling blood. "Ho, boy! That's the spirit!" the Redneck celebrated. Everyone watching winced.

"He's dying like a dog, man!" the Caucasian yelled.

George's arms and legs continued to thrash as he gripped his gushing throat, bug-eyed.

"Put him out of his misery!" the Blonde next to Haggert pleaded.

The Redneck considered this with a nod, then calmly shot George in the head. His skull erupted.

More chilling silence.

The Caucasian was pinching the bridge of his nose, while Sy grit his teeth, chest heaving. The Brunette stood poker-faced in gunsmoke; she dropped the revolver to the floor.

"Let me ask you something," the Redneck addressed Sharon. "You didn't even bat an eye. You punched George's ticket and didn't even *think* about it. Why him? Why not Sy?"

"I don't like Blacks. You asked, so I answered," Sharon replied in a low, grating voice. She pulled up her sleeve and displayed a tattoo that read: ARYAN NATION: WHITE IS MIGHT.

Haggert was surprised.

"Well how do you like that?" the Redneck said. "One of those white supremacists." He belted out a laugh. "Don't that beat all? But, wait a minute. You guys hate Jews too, right?"

"Yeah," Sharon answered in the stone-cold voice. "We just hate Blacks more."

The Redneck's grin beamed; he quickly picked up the revolver and put a new bullet in the cylinder. Haggert thought he knew what was coming.

"You heard that, Sy. She hates you too." The Redneck gave Sy the Revolver, while holding his other gun to Sy's head. "Show us what you're made of . . ."

BAM!

Sy hit Sharon square in the forehead. She went down as if struck by a truck.

BAM!

The Redneck shot Sy in the temple.

The Blonde shuddered next to Haggert. The Caucasian simply stood there below the television. "Would somebody please tell me what's going on here?" he said. "I don't know what's happening. You're killing everybody."

"I'm making my statement, that's what's happening."

"In an odd way," Haggert began, "it's all about hatred, isn't it?"

Everybody looked at Haggert's bizarre comment.

"They say love makes the world go round, but that's not really true. Hatred does. Look at what's going on here. Look closely. Sharon hated George because he was black, Sy hated Sharon because she's a supremacist, Mahhad hated—what did he say?—all the deliberate enemies of Islam. That's a lot of hatred. And remember what we just saw on the TV? Bombings, war, flood gates dynamited, radioactive materials being stolen. Hatred everywhere you look. It almost seems like it's part of a process."

"What process?" the Caucasian asked. "What are you talking about? It's all either mental illness or environment."

"Yes, like a disease. But disease, in actuality, is part of a natural process. It controls the population, gives germs and viruses a means of support–something else always lives off what dies." Haggert meant it. "Maybe hatred functions in the same way. We see it as something very human and something very negative. But maybe it's just part of the way things are supposed to be."

The Redneck frowned. "If you're trying to be a fucking philosopher, you're fucking up. I don't know what the hell you're talking about."

"Seriously," Haggert elaborated. "Why can't hatred be part of the natural order? Like an earthquake or a hurricane, like a mudslide. Like the Black Death of the Middle Ages, or cholera, or the meteor that exterminated the dinosaurs. Hatred, too. If it's part of nature, then that means it's part of the natural order."

"I just came in here because I wanted to get shitfaced," the Blonde said. "But instead I get to listen to this crap in the middle of a mass murder. Hating people isn't *natural*."

"Don't feel bad, honey," the Caucasian added. "I don't know what he's talking about either."

Haggert smiled. "I understand, but it's a consideration, isn't it? Maybe chaos is part of evolvement, and hatred contributes to that just like a natural disaster. You can only go so far before you have to start over again."

"The world's a bunch of shit because of the people in it," the Redneck asserted, "not because of nature, for shit's sake."

"All right, good. I believe you're right. The world *is* a bunch of shit. Maybe it's time to start over again. Maybe, in some weird way, we're all part of that." Haggert looked right at the Redneck. "Maybe *you're* part of that."

"What? By killing innocent people?" the Caucasian interrupted. "That's ridiculous. I hate people too, I hate *a lot* of people. Things are *never* as they seem, people are *never* as they seem. They let you think you're important to them, and *that's* when they either pull the cord on you, write you off, or stab you in the back. I've been getting trashed, lied to, ripped off, and flushed down the toilet by people for my whole life, and I'm so sick of it I could bend over and throw up my heart. I think my hatred is legitimate because most people aren't. But you know what? I still don't want to *kill* any of them."

BAM!

The bullet blew out the back of the Caucasian's head. He actually stood for a moment more, staring. Then he collapsed.

"You *should've* killed them, asshole," the Redneck said to the body. "'Cos look at you now."

The television fluttered in the background. Haggert could hear the Blonde's heart beating. She looked nauseous, and Haggert felt nauseous too. "An interesting night, wouldn't you say?" he remarked.

"Yeah, *damn* interesting," the Redneck agreed. He wiped sweat off his brow. The air smelled gritty.

"Are you happy with your statement so far?" Haggert asked.

"Sure, but I'm not part of any *natural order*, I'll tell you that." The Redneck looked at the last wallet on the table. "Maria," he said to the stunning Blonde. "That's a nice name."

Maria's shoulders were drooping.

"Bet you wish you never walked into *this* bar tonight, huh? Some happy hour!" The Redneck chuckled, stuffing bills in his pocket. "Shit, I forgot somebody, didn't I?"

He put the gun right against Haggert's forehead.

"Wallet."

Haggert gave it to him.

"Let's see, let's see. Wow, that's a lot of money," the Redneck commented, pulling out a sheaf. "Richard Edwin Haggert . . ." Then he paused, squinting. "Feeling sick, Richard?"

Haggert smiled. "I've felt better; it's not everyday I get taken hostage. But there are other circumstances, too. Circumstances that you're not aware of. Of course not. How could you be?"

"Huh?"

Haggert let out a wearied breath. "It's part of a natural order. Hatred. Everyone's. Mine, yours. I'm afraid I've got you beat, though."

"What are you babbling about now, buddy?"

"All my identification is in the wallet that you're holding. Did you look at them all?"

A long face as the Redneck scrutinized the cards.

"And think back," Haggert added. "Something we heard on the news a little while ago . . . Something rather important. Remember?"

The Redneck's eyes narrowed on the next ID card. "Wait a minute, yeah . . ."

Haggert used the moment of distraction well. From his jacket he withdrew a M950 .380 machine pistol, compact in spite of the 100-round helical magazine. One squeeze ripped off a dozen rounds into the Redneck's belly, behind a quick sputtering sound, like a lawnmower.

Maria shrieked, flinching, a hand to her heart.

The stream of empty brass casings tinkled against the floor. The Redneck collapsed dead on top of George and Sy's bodies.

Maria was nearly paralyzed in bewilderment and shock, her lower lip trembling. "What in God's name is going on?

You had the gun the whole time, but you didn't use it till now? You could've saved all these people!"

Another tired breath. "You don't understand, Maria— but you will, at least I hope so." Haggert fingered the odd boxy firearm. "It's all about hatred. It's all relative. It's more effective to let someone else's hatred work for me, to my own end. And I truly believe it *is* part of a natural order. I was on my way to Washington tonight, but there was an accident on Route 50. That's why I pulled in here. I know, now, I'll never make it to Washington. I thought I could, but I was wrong. The potassium iodide pills only work so well. I'm dying."

Maria eyes looked bottomless as she stared at him.

A few strands of hair fell out of Haggert's head. "I'm dying of radiation poisoning. See?" He pointed to his ID card that the Redneck had dropped. Maria's wide eyes dropped from Haggert's face to the card, that read in bold letters: RICHARD EDWIN HAGGERT, SEC/RADMAT CLEARANCE LEVEL 4 - MATERIAL DISPOSAL TECHNICIAN, CALVERT CLIFFS NPP.

Maria was thinking back to the news, her face paling. "The nuclear power plant," she droned. "They said somebody stole something . . ."

"Um-hmm. Me. I took one gallon of fuel-rod waste water, laced with powdered Cesium-137. I mixed it into 300 pounds of an ammonia-based explosive compound called RDX, and let it dry. It's in the trunk of my car right now, fitted with blasting caps. They call it a radiological dispersion charge, a 'dirty nuke.' On a night like this? Streets full of Christmas shoppers? It'll kill hundreds now, and quadruple local cancer rates, and all of downtown Annapolis will be rendered uninhabitable for the next fifty years."

"Why?" Maria mouthed.

"Because it's part of the natural order, Maria."

Haggert doubted that she felt much pain when he ripped ten rounds into her head. The casings chimed to the floor.

He stood up with a smile despite the dull pain. More hair fell out as he trudged to the back door. Haggert felt confident that he'd make it back to the Lincoln before he died.

GODDESS OF THE NEW DARK AGE

"What is real?" he wondered aloud.

Then Smith heard the words: *Revere me. Make me real.* Not his words, but a muffled hiss, like someone whispering on the other side of the wall . . .

The wall was nightmare: tremoring flesh, skin sweating in turmoil, pain, despair. *So I'm dreaming standing up now,* Smith thought. *Wide awake, in daylight.*

Flecks of mica guttered up from the sidewalk. The sun raged. *Old man,* he thought. City police cruised by, eyeing him, squab faces dark behind tinted glass. "Frog, Ice, Cokesmoke?" a hand-pocketed black man asked him. By a newspaper stand, where headlines blared MAN SETS WIFE & CHILDREN ON FIRE, a raddled prostitute twitched, scratching at needlemarks inside of her thigh. In the mouth of a urine-soaked alley, a woman in rags vomited up blood as rats the size of small puppies boldly approached the emesis, to eat.

Smith hated the sun. It seemed bright with life, which made him feel even older, more depleted. *Where am I going?* The question didn't mean now, today, this minute. *Where am I going forever?* he wondered. *Where have I been?*

The footsteps padded behind him; they had for weeks. Smith had long since stopped looking back. It sounded

57

like someone walking barefoot—a woman, he surmised, a robust, beautiful woman. He also detected the lovely scent—perfume—and some kind of inexplicable heat at his groin and his heart. Whenever he turned, though, at the sound and the lush fragrance, nothing was there. Just a shadow sometimes, just a fleck, like the mica in the cement.

Perhaps it was a ghost, whatever ghosts were. *Ghost, or just hallucination.* Smith's physical body felt like vermiculated meat. Too many artificial sweeteners, cigarettes, alcohol, saturated fats. A body could only take so much vandalism. But Smith didn't care. Why should he, now? Or ever, for that matter?

Or maybe ghosts were real. *Physical residuum,* he speculated. *Interplanar leakage.* Was there really a netherworld, like an anxious tongue licking across pressed lips, desperate for entry? He'd read somewhere that horror left a stain, a laceration through which the tenants of the void could ooze into the world. But if this were true, mankind would surely be smothered by such ooze.

So what was this "ghost?" A spirit? An angel?

Was the ghost real?

Sometimes he could actually see it, via the presage: the longing perfume scent, the warmth. Generally only at night. *Of course,* he thought. *Night.* Dr. Greene had told him to expect as much. But ghosts? "Be prepared for some containdications from the chemotherapy," came the words like a clipped dissertation. "Olfactory and aural hallucinosis. Exodikinesis, immoderate scotipic debris, synaptic maladaption and toxicity intolerance. It's normal." *Normal,* Smith reflected. *Dying's normal too.* Three treatments left him racked for hours, dry heaving bile. His hair had fallen out. "To hell with this," he'd told Greene, on the fourth visit. "Let me die." Cancer seemed an appropriate way for a writer to die. It seemed nearly allegorical. The festering beneath the miraculous veneer of human flesh.

No, the ghost wasn't a side effect. *It must be real.* He thought he could see it, the shadow within the shadow, peering back. A shadow in want of flesh.

Was it Smith's flesh it wanted? *Why should it want me? My flesh's dying. I am essentially a walking corpse.* He could smell the perfume, even over the city's mephitis of carbon-monoxide, stale sweat, and garbage. "You smell beautiful," he whispered. "Whoever you are." He walked on, shriveling against the glare of the sun, but then stopped to look back once more.

"Are you real?" he asked.

"What is real?" Smith lit a cigarette; it scarcely mattered now. But the question kept occurring to him, like an itching rash. Why should it be so important?

His biopsy analysis—now *that* was real. The single sheet seemed too thin for such a grievous message. It drooped in his hand like something already dead:

CYTOLOGY REPORT
NAME: Smith, Gerald E.
AGE: 61, W/M
CLINICAL CONSULTATION: Large Cell Coaxial Mass
Specify: <u>Right Lung Mass Aspirate</u>
_ Negative
_ Atypical
<u>X</u> Positive

MICROSCOPIC DESCRIPTION: Right Lung Aspirate showing numerous malignant large cells, some of which showing large vesicular irregular nuclei, consistent with non-keratinizing carcinoma, probably large-cell differentiated type of adenocarcinoma.

PATHOLOGY DIAGNOSIS: Positive for Malignant Cells.

Smith was a realist. *No sense in crying over a spilt life.*
He felt he had a mission now, but wasn't sure what it could
be. He couldn't stop thinking of the ghost.

"Are you real?"

Behind his typewriter, behind his desk, a shadow, or a
smudge, seemed to nod. "Who are you!" Smith suddenly
yelled. "What do you want from me?"

Your reckoning, something seemed to hiss. It wasn't even
really a sound, more akin to insect appendages abrading. The
soft bare footfalls followed him to the bathroom. *A ghost
is coming into the toilet with me,* he thought. It was almost
funny. He smiled at the lovely perfume-scent, then winced,
urinating blood. Of course: by now the disease had bloomed.
Dr. Greene had warned him, hadn't he? "Renal malfunction.
What happens, Mr. Smith, is that the raging malignant cells
become insinuated into the nephrons and the cortical kidney
tissue, scleroticizing the calyx cavities." *Charming,* Smith
thought now. The pain was extraordinary, like bright light.

Smith had been a writer for over forty years. *Had been,*
he emphasized, pulling up his zipper. He flushed the toilet,
and thought of his career. Had he been a good writer?
He'd thought so, until Greene had told him the truth. The
good doctor had at least been respectful enough of Smith's
profession not to mince words. "You're dying," he'd said.
"You'll be gone in oh, say, six weeks."

Gone, Smith considered. He was still in the bathroom.
What did *gone* mean? Did it mean no longer real? The
question continued to nag at him, worse than the cancer.
"What is real?" he asked.

Find out, the hiss replied. *You haven't much time.*

As a writer, he'd spent his life trying to create realities
out of assessments of imagination. *The truth of any story
can only exist in its bare words,* he'd heard someone say in
a bar when he was eighteen. He'd been a writer ever since,

60

pursuing that. But now, now that he was dying, he knew that he'd failed utterly. Was that why the ghost had come to him, evoked by the knowledge of his failure? What was the hiss trying to tell him?

"I see you," he said. For a moment he had, behind him in the mirror. *Beautiful,* he thought. A beautiful, beautiful woman, an amalgam composed of inverted bits of wallpaper, a prolapsation. It smiled weakly, then vanished. Only its pleasant smell remained.

The television poured forth atrocities. Or were they realities? "Up next," promised the newswoman with a visage of wood, "Florida state supreme court grants local journalists the right to televise executions." Outside the courthouse, a crowd in floodlit darkness cheered. Then, a commercial, a slim brunette in a white swimsuit: "If you're counting calories, here's something you should know . . ." Smith changed the channel. ". . .where officials estimate that one thousand children are starving to death daily, while government troops remain free to confiscate relief rations from the United Red Cross, selling what they don't eat themselves to the black market."

And next: "—confessed today to that he knowingly tainted the entire hospital's transfusion supply with AIDS infected bl—"

"—amid allegations of abducting over one hundred children for what the FBI officials have called 'the underground snuff-film circuit—"

"—strangled slowly with a lampcord while her common-law husband and his friends took turns—"

Smith turned off the set, feeling as confused as he felt disgusted. The newspaper offered more of the same. CRACKMOM TURNS KIDS TO PROSTITUTES read one local headline. The *Post* seemed less blunt: EARTHQUAKE DEATH TOLL EXPECTED TO REACH 120,000. Here was

61

a story. A Tucson, Arizona, woman locked her three children in her attic while she went shopping with a friend. All three children died as the temperature in the attic exceeded 150 degrees. Stray bullets in a drug-related shootout killed three six-year-olds in front of a Detroit apartment project. The body of a thirteen-year old girl was found by hunters in Davidsonville, Maryland; the police reported that she'd been raped en mass and tortured with power tools. A suitcase was discovered in a dumpster behind a Washington D.C. convenience store, containing a dead newborn baby complete with umbilical and placenta.

Smith's contemplations wavered. What could be more real than all of this? *But there must be something.* The ghost was walking around; he could feel it. It seemed to be perusing the bookshelf full of his work. Then it hissed at him, and disappeared.

The sun felt like a blade against his face as his guest dragged him back out onto the street. He was shriveling. It occurred to him, as he ascended the stone steps, that this was the first time he'd entered a church since he'd become a writer.

An old priest limped across the chancel, his bald head like a shiny ball of dough. He began to change the frontals on the altar.

"Excuse me, sir . . . er, Father," Smith interrupted.

"Yes?"

"What is real?"

The priest straightened, a frocked silhouette before stained glass. He did not question, or even pause upon, the obscurity of Smith's query. He answered at once: "God, Christ, the kingdom of Heaven."

"But how do you know?"

The priest's bland face smiled. He held up his Bible.

Smith thanked him and walked out. He felt abandoned,

not as much by God as by himself. Conviction wasn't proof. Belief didn't validate a *reality.* Next, he took a Yellow to the University, where the static sunlight made everything look brittle and fake. Inside, cool darkness and tile shine led him down the hall. PHILOSOPHY DEPARTMENT. Smith stepped unannounced into the first office. A man—who looked as old—glanced up from a cluttered industrial gray metal desk. "May I . . . *help* you?"

Smith considered how he must look—a haggard, emaciated vagabond. "Forgive my appearance . . ." *but it's hard to look good when you're dying from a large-cell metastatic mass.* He had no time for intricate explanations nor cordialities. "I have a question that only a philosopher can answer. The question is this: What is real?"

The professor lit a pipe with a face engraved in relief on the bowl. His eyes looked tiny below the great, bushy gray brows. "That's quite a universal question, wouldn't you say? You want *my* opinion?"

In the window, the campus stood empty in sunlight. "Yes," Smith said after a pause. That's when he noticed the ghost. It was standing just outside, looking at him, an ethereal chaperon. "Yes, yes," he said. "I'd appreciate your opinion very much."

"Ah, what is real?" Pipe smoke smeared the professor's aged face. "Consider, first, the initial tenets of conclusionary nihilism. Truth is reality, and there is no objective basis for truth. Take mathematics for example, which exists only because space and time are forms of intuition; all material qualities are only the *outward* appearances arising from monadistic nexi. See? What is real can only be found in the *im*material mind; hence, the solipsistic doctrine. The human self is the only thing, in other words, that can be known and therefore verified. Quite a contradiction, since life is clearly a material, or a physio-chemical, interaction.

63

Being and reality are not found in objects of knowledge but in something accessible only to the free and total self. Man's destiny is a struggle for power, or, in your case, for answers. What I mean is, the real can never be made manifest in our finite minds but in the genetic empiricism beyond the whole. In other words, and I think it should be obvious now, reality is a consistence of a judgment pursuant to other judgements, fitting in ultimately to a single absolute system."

Smith resisted rolling his eyes. He thanked the professor for his time, and left, thinking, *what a crock of shit.*

So it wasn't truth, and it wasn't spirit. Smith lit a cigarette, pondering the smoke. *Love?* he wondered. Was love real? Did love make something real? He didn't know. He'd been too busy writing to ever love anyone.

These were simply subjectivities trying to be concrete, which was impossible. *Beauty, then?* He leaned back. *Hmmm.* Did beauty—a true subjectivity—make something real? Suddenly Smith felt buoyant with excitement. His kidneys throbbed, and his lung felt like a bleeding clot. Yet the surmise gave him energy.

Beauty.

Wasn't beauty what all writers were supposed to pursue?

He heard a sigh, or no—a *hiss.* Did it denote relief, or disappointment? "It's beauty, isn't it?" Smith asked aloud to the shadow which now lingered at the closet. Was it inspecting his clothes? The shape sharpened as dusk bled into the room, creeping. What had it said, just days ago, on the street? *Revere me.* Smith knew at once that he must appease the ghost, with aphorism, with comprehension. "I'll show you," he said.

He opened the Yellow Pages, to the E's. ESCORTS UNLIMITED, BEAUTIFUL GIRLS, CONFIDENTIAL, 24 HOURS, VISA, MASTERCARD.

The sigh replayed in his head, and the wondrous scent rose as Smith reached for the phone, to call beauty.

"Do you believe in ghosts?"

The girl's smile twitched. "Uh, well . . ."

"Never mind," Smith said. "I was allegorizing, I suppose. I used to be a novelist." He sat behind his desk, behind his typewriter, which was turned off. He would never turn it on again, and this left him dryly depressed. He had nothing to write. But it seemed a suitable place from which to observe: the lap of his failure. *I've written over a hundred books,* he felt inclined to brag. But so what? Why say that? His books had not been real.

"What, uh, what would you like me to do?" the girl inquired.

Smith squinted. "I want to see you. I realize how obscure that must sound, but I'm on a quest of sorts, and I'm afraid I've become subject to a considerable time constraint. I've been made aware of a possibility, though, quite recently, that reality only arrives through an acknowledgment, or a reckoning, of human beauty. Not an objective acknowledgment, but a temporal one. I'm looking for something, the underside perhaps, or what makes something real in our minds and, more critically, our hearts. Use a sentence in fiction as an example. Objectively, the sentence is nothing more than configurations of ink on a piece of paper. But the mechanism of the words, and *function* of the mechanism, in conjunction with the manner by which we define the sequence of the words, affects a transposition of imagery. It makes the sentence real in the process. The *process*—do you understand?" Smith doubted that she did. "The words suddenly become *real,* in some other, ineffable way." He must sound worse than the professor. *You're just a piece of physical meat,* he could have put it, more simply. *But I need to see what you are beyond that, not as just a body but as an image transposed* through *the body.* Would it offend her? Would she understand?

At least the ghost seemed to understand. Smith caught frequent glimpses now, since the call-girl had arrived. He felt certain that the more effectively he strove to conquer the question—What is real?—the more real the ghost would become.

"I smell perfume," the girl remarked.

"Yes," Smith said but did not elaborate. "In other words, I merely need to see you, all of you."

"Ah," the girl said, stretching the word. "Now I get it. Now I know what you mean." She smiled, a manufactured wickedness, and took off the short fuchsia dress. "You just want to watch. That's okay. It's your dime."

Smith's "dime," in this case, had been a $150 escort fee on his charge card, plus "tip." He'd given her several hundred in cash, all he had left in the apartment. What did he need money for? He'd never really needed it in life. What good would it do him now?

"Show me your beauty," Smith said.

Off, then, came the garters, the stockings and frilly lace bra, all the same vibrant, bright fuchsia. She wore no panties. What stood before Smith now was her raw, physical reality. But— *Not enough,* he thought, squinting past his desk. He needed to see her *beauty,* and at first she did indeed strike him as beautiful . . .

Smith tipped up the desklamp. "Come closer. Please. Closer to the desk."

She sauntered forward like a chic model on a runway, and assumed quick poses, turning before the light. Flesh flashed in cold glare. Glance by glance, the beauty collapsed.

The silken white-blond hair and bangs clashed with the

waxed, black pubic patch. The rhinoplastied nose seemed too perfect on the elegant face. Smith's eyes calculated up the sleek supple physique, and snagged. Minute cannula marks pocked along her trim hips and waist, from liposuction, and when she raised her arms, the erect orbs of her breasts easily displayed the hairline implant scars.

She blinked at him, her smile freezing. Even the crystal-blue eyes were a lie, designer contacts.

"Thank you," Smith said. "You may go now."

Her nude, pretty shoulders shrugged. "It's your dime." Then she quickly put her clothes back on and left.

The ghost was laughing.

On the night he was to die, Smith awakened as if rising from a lime pit. The darkness swarmed. His eyes felt plucked open by fish hooks.

You should have more faith, the hiss whispered.

"I figured as much," he muttered. He walked to his desk, wizened as a dried corpse in the moonlight. *Faith?* he wondered. Smith didn't believe in God. Perhaps he should have. Nevertheless, he doubted that the ghost meant religious faith.

Faith in me. Faith in what is real.

He'd failed again, he'd misconstrued everything. He'd never know reality now, only the reality of death, of being embalmed and buried, of dissolving to slime in a box. But what was he—a writer—really dying of? Cancer, or the failure to recognize what was real? Prevarications were killing him, not disease.

Deserts, he thought. *Wastelands. All the lies of history.*

Only two realities mattered now. His dying flesh, and the ghost.

He saw it more clearly now than ever, which made sense. It faced the window, naked in its oblivion, a razorline shape of inverted oddments of darkness and light. "You're real, aren't you?" Smith stated more than asked.

Only you can make me real, the hiss replied.

Smith felt adrift on the scent of her—or its—perfume. But how could he *make* it real? Did it mean that it was only half-real now? Did it mean there was something about *Smith* that could unloose the ghost's full reality?

"Assimilation?" Smith lit a cigarette, his last. "No," he felt. "Transposition." Perhaps he'd been correct all along, back when he'd been talking to the blonde call-girl. Correct, but on the wrong tangent. It was his trade that had summoned the ghost—he was a writer, a creator, or, more accurately, a *re*creator. Writers re-recreated their own conceptions of images of reality and blended them with abstraction, *transposing* the images, and making both the conception and the abstraction, in a sense—

Real, he thought.

He'd only been partly right. Beauty reflected only a semantic; it was something created, not transposed. Smith stared at the shifting figure and its ebon glint. It seemed to gaze back at him, over the shadow-boned shoulder . . .

"Too late, though, hmmm?" Of course. His life was over. His face felt sucked in. The old heart began to skip within the sunken cage of his chest. But at least he would die pondering this; at least he would die trying.

Ghosts. Not Dickensian specters flailing chains and moaning amid graveyards. Not transparent apparitions and sheet-shapes. Ghosts would be entities of human backwash, of unfulfillment, of failure. Ghosts would be slivers of the real world. And what was the world, then? A realm, not a sphere of rock, a domain of . . . transposition—a mutable domain, one that squirmed with each new generation, and each new age.

The ghost turned. Its black-chasm eyes widened.

"Now I've got you going, eh?" Smith felt proud. "The old dying stick in the mud isn't as dumb as you thought."

Make me real, came the hushed reverberation.

"I don't know how," Smith testily replied.

But you do.

Was it weeping? It seemed to be, perhaps as Smith, secretly, had wept over his entire life. He turned on the radio. Vivaldi seemed nice to die to, or a light nocturne by Field. Besides, Smith wanted beautiful music as he confronted the ghost.

He rose, joints clicking, as he crossed the nighted room, atrophied, shrivel-penised, and as pale as death already. He could feel the cancer percolating, and it was a surprisingly neutral sensation. *Transposition,* he considered. *Each new generation, each new age.* Yes, the world was a realm of emotion, of which this queer thing in his room had surely been born. Behind him, out of the dark, the radio squawked another day's unholy news. A bomb had exploded on an airliner, scattering hundreds of bodies across the outskirts of Los Angeles. A coterie of scientists convened in Washington, citing the benefits of using brain tissue from aborted fetuses for genetic research. Terrorists had thrown seven satchel charges into an Israeli maternity ward . . .

Look. The ghost indicated the window. Smith peered out. At first, what he saw seemed beautiful: a warm endless night chipped by stars, the high, resplendent moon, and man's crisp, perfectly symmetrical monuments. The scape of buildings looked like an intricate carved mesa of flawless black, still with tiny lights.

"It's beautiful," Smith muttered.

But then its reality rose before the vision. Flashing red and blue lights of terror. Sirens. Gunshots. Distant screams. A cool breeze carried in the chaotic stench.

Smith blinked.

Revere me. Make me real.

The ghost shifted. Now he understood.

It's time now, isn't it? Time for a new realm? Your realm is done, isn't it?

It didn't mean his life—of course not. It meant the *age*.

The night lolled. The ghost shifted like black sand pouring, until it was perfect, beautiful flesh. Dark long straight hair and dark eyes. Dark yet lambent nakedness. Poreless indefectible skin smooth as newly spun silk. And it wasn't a woman at all, but a girl, a prepubescent little girl. Nor was it a ghost . . .

A goddess, Smith realized. *A little goddess . . .*

The goddess' voice eddied like water running through the bowels of a sewer, or garbage blown in gutters.

The new dark age needs a scribe.

Smith felt on fire inside. He watched his hand reach out, but it wasn't the veined, liver-spotted hand he had known. It was a new hand, forged in truth, in acknowledgment. Smith wept, oblivious to the new hot blood, the fresh skin, strong muscles, and steady heart. He embraced the goddess.

He began to slide down, as if on a greased pole, sloughing off her perfect skin, and revealing her true age. Her horror sang to him, and embraced him back, the flensed figure gleaming in hate, disease, insanity. In despair and in pus. In cruelty. In truth.

Smith knelt in worship, and kissed the little feet, which were now caked by the blood, offal, and excrement of eons.

HANDS

When the EMTs brought the guy in, it looked like he must've sat down in a bathtub full of blood. "Damn it!" Parker shouted, thinking *I'm off duty in five minutes! I ain't got time for a cut-down!*

Dr. Parker was completely bald; he was also in charge of Emergency Room Cove 4 tonight, and had been for the last twelve hours–or make that eleven hours and fifty-five minutes. He was pulling noon-to-mids for eight days straight, but he had tomorrow off. It would sure be nice to just go home and get some sleep, but this bleeder looked like a two-or three-hour string-job at least.

"Don't forget your Hippocratic Oath," Moler, his intern, remarked with a mordant grin. Moler had a short beard and a wise ass. "Looks like you miss Jerry springer tonight, daddy-o."

"Just get the meat on the table," Parker ordered. He smirked as Moler and the gurney-jockey hoisted the unmoving patient up onto the crash table. "What's the guy's stats, Ben Casey?" he asked the EMT.

The EMT gave him the finger. "Looks like a single GS high and inside of the right thigh. We slapped a tourniquet on and brought him in."

"Don't EMTs have to go to school anymore?" Parker said. "How come you didn't ligate the wound in the ambulance?"

"Because we picked him up on Jackson Street, about two minutes away, Dr. Dickhead," the EMT replied.

These fuckin' meat-wagon jocks, Parker thought. *They got no respect for doctors anymore.*

"All that blood?" Moler observed. "The bullet might've hit the femoral artery."

"Duh," Parker said. "At least the Two Stooges out there know how to strap a tourniquet."

"The guy's type is A-pos, Shemp," the EMT added. "Have fun. I'm out of here."

"Thanks for staying to help out," Parker shot back.

"Hey, that shit's your job, I just drive. You're the guy getting a hundred and fifty k a year. Have fun."

The EMT left. *Eat shit and die,* Parker thought.

"We need three pints of A-pos in C4, stat," Moler said into the phone and hung up. Then he leaned over the victim, squinting at the blood-drenched groin. "Looks small, looks like someone popped him with a .25, maybe a .32. Aimed for his cock but missed by an inch."

Close but no cigar. Parker snapped on Tru-Touch sterile gloves. "They picked him up on Jackson, at this hour? He's probably a john, picked up a hooker, got rough, so she shot him." Parker got them all the time. "Can't say I blame her."

"Probably right—"

A draft wafted. The cove door swung open, and it was the EMT again. "Oh, and I forgot to tell ya. We checked the guy's wallet when we picked him up–he's a homicide captain with city PD."

"Move it!" Parker yelled. "Fuck!"

But Moler was shaking his head. "Come on–the guy's dying."

"I don't want a damn *cop* dying on my table! Get the hemos and the shears! We're doing a cut-down right now!"

Shiny instruments clinked; Moler rushed the tray over,

then raised the pair of Sistrunk-brand German fabric shears. Parker put on his monocular, a plastic headset sort of thing with a single lens fitting over the eye; he'd need it to see the broken arterial walls. The completely bald head, along with the monocular, made Parker look like a Nazi mad scientist.

Once the wound was exposed, he would cut laterally along the femoral artery and with a nearly microscopic needle and thread, perform a pre-op ligature in order to effect a cessation of the arterial blood flow. "Go!" he shouted. "Cut his pants off!"

"Roger that," Moler said. The shears cut right through the waist of the slacks and the leather belt like onionskin paper.

Parker turned momentarily, snapped up an Arista scalpel. Its stainless-steel flash winked at him in the overheads. But before he could turn back around to the patient, he heard Moler's dismal mutter.

"Oh, shit—"

"What!" Parker barked. "Don't tell me he 64'd!"

"Naw, but . . . You better take a look at this. I think we got the guy they've been writing about in the papers . . ."

Dr. Parker finished turning. He closed the eye over which the monocular rested and looked down with his other eye. Moler had indeed expertly cut the patient's pants off with the shears, and the boxer shorts as well. And when Parker saw what lay there, he knew immediately what his intern meant.

The "patient" had been carrying a severed human hand in his undershorts.

I guess I knew Jameson was the one the moment after the police shrink explained the psychiatric profile. But what tagged it was when Jameson took me to his Belltown condo and showed me those pictures. He introduced me to his wife, then showed me the row of framed snapshots over the mantle. One was a picture of him as a child, his father's arm around him.

But no mother.

The lack of the facilitation of a nurturing touch . . .

My name's Matt Hauge; I'm a crime reporter for the *Seattle Times.* The other papers were calling the killer the "Handyman," and I guess that's why Captain Jay Jameson had come to me in the first place. A couple weeks ago, he walked right into my office and said, "I need your help."

This was a cop, one of the bigwigs–a captain up for deputy chief. Cops generally hated press people but here's this tall, imposing guy flashing his shield in my face and asking *me* for help.

"This Handyman shit—that's my case," he said. .

"It's my case too," I countered.

"Yeah. That's why I'm here." He sat down, pulled out a cigarette, asked if I minded if he smoked, then lit up before I could answer. Now that I think back, I should've known even then. This guy *looked* like a perv. He had lines down his face like a James Street speed freak. One eye looked a teeny bit higher than the other. And he had this weird dirty blond hair spiked with grey and a tan, roughened complexion like a waterman. He didn't look like a cop. He looked like a killer.

"I know it's your case," he said. "You think I'm here for shits and giggles?"

"Pardon me, Captain?" I said.

"Every newspaper in the goddamn *state* is printing all this tabloid shit about the case. They're making me look like the most incompetent cop in the history of the department. And this 'Handyman' tagline they're pushing? It sounds ridiculous, and it makes *me* look ridiculous." Jameson got up, closed my office door, then returned to his seat. Plumes of cigarette smoke seemed to follow him around like lingering spirits. "What is it with press people anyway?" he said next. Then the son of a bitch tapped an ash on my carpet. "The first thing you do is accuse the police of inefficiency, and then you gotta slap these horror-movie taglines onto any repeat crime you can get your hands on."

"It's a way of increasing the identifiability of the event to a mass readership, because it helps sell papers. But I might remind you, Captain–before you flick more ashes on my floor–that I'm one journalist who's never used that tagline and has never criticized the police in their efforts to catch the killer."

"Yeah. That's why I like you."

By the way, the so-called "Handyman" Case involved a fairly recent sequence of murders in the downtown area. Three women so far: two known street prostitutes and one homeless woman. All three had been found strangled to death, their bodies carefully hidden along the Jackson Street corridor. And all three had been found with both of their hands missing. Cut off with an ax or a hatchet.

"And don't worry about your floor," he went on. "What? Your big paper can't afford janitors?"

"Captain Jameson, for a man coming in here asking for help, you might need to learn a few lessons in sincerity."

"Oh, fuck that shit. Don't be a creamcake. The only good journalism about this case that I've seen has been written by you. I want to make a deal."

"A deal? For what?"

"There've been more than three girls. That info's gonna get leaked eventually. I want you to break it first. I'll tell you everything about the case the press *hasn't* heard. You'll look good."

"Yes sir, I guess I would," I realized. "But what's the catch?"

"You make me look good along the way. You write for

the most respectable paper in the city. All I'm asking is for some slack. I give you the goods, but when you write it, you say my unit's doing its best. And when we catch this fuck-up . . . you put in a good word for me. Deal?"

"No deal," I said. "You're bribing me. You've got balls coming in here telling me this. I'm a newspaper reporter for God's sake!"

"I wouldn't call it bribery." Jameson showed a big toothy grin, then flicked more ashes on the floor. "That descrambler you got? Sounds smalltime, but did you know it's now an FCC first-degree misdemeanor? A federal crime? Get'cha a year in jail and a five-grand fine for starters. Then let's talk about your Schedule C deductions. Newspaper writers with freelance gigs on the side? You pay Miscellaneous income tax, right? Those pseudonymous articles you wrote for *The Stranger, The Rocket,* and *Mansplat?*"

You son of a bitch, I thought.

"Can we talk?" Jameson asked.

Seattle's never been a city known for its crime rate. Thirty-six murders last year in the entire Seattle-Metro area. Compare that to L.A., New York, Washington D.C. and at least a dozen others tipping a thousand. What we're known for instead is the Space Needle, the Monorail, and the largest fish depot in the hemisphere. Microsoft and Boeing. Happy times and happy people. Low unemployment, and no state income tax. No partisan politics and no potholes. And more NEA and college grants per-capita than any major metropolis in the country.

A good place to live.

But then there's the downside that no one sees. Higher temperatures in the winter and wide-open welfare policies wag false promises to the destitute–it's a magnet to the hopeless. They come here looking for the yellow-brick road but all they get is another bridge to sleep under, another dumpster to eat out of. Just take a walk around Third and James, Yesler Street, the trolley bridge on Jackson. You'll see them trudging back and forth on their journey to nowhere. Stick-figures in rags, ghosts not quite incorporeal yet. Their dead eyes sunk into wax faces and bloodless lips asking for change or promising anything you want for twenty dollars. There are so many of them here, so many of these non-people with no names, no backgrounds, no lives.

The perfect grist of a psycho-killer.

"Our total's sixteen so far," Jameson admitted. "But that's not even the worst consideration—"

"God knows how many others are out there you *haven't* found," I said.

"You got it."

Jameson had brought me to his office at the city district headquarters. A large tack-board hung on the wall with sixteen pieces of paper pinned to it. Each piece of paper showed a victim's name, or in several cases just the letters *No ID* and a recovery date.

"How'd you manage to keep it quiet for so long?" I asked.

"Luck, mostly," Jameson grumbled. "Until recently, we'd find one here, one there. Isolated incidents, the victims were all nobodies: hookers, street trash. And we have our ways of keeping stuff away from the press."

"So you knew about this all along," I said, not asked.

"Yeah, for over three years." He was standing by the window, staring out as he talked. "Every single police department in the area is still the laughing stock over the Green River thing. What could we do? Have another one of those?"

"That's not the point, is it?"

He turned, a tight sarcastic smile on his face like a razor

slash. "You fuckin' press guys. My job's to protect the residents of this city. It's not gonna do me or them any good if they find out this shit's been going on for years."

"And the victims?"

"So what? I don't give a shit about a bunch of whores and crackheads. I don't work for them–I work for the real people. And it sure as shit doesn't help when you press people bend over backwards to trash the police. If you're not complaining about increased burglary rates you're complaining about kids buying cigarettes. It's all our fault, huh? The police aren't doing enough."

I almost laughed at his insolence.

Jameson winced. "I'm just generalizing so don't be an asshole. Fuck, I'm forty-nine years old, been breaking my ass out there since I was a nineteen-year-old cadet. I'm a shoe-in for deputy chief, then all of a sudden a couple of dead junkies make the papers, and there goes my promotion."

"So this is all about you," I said. "You're just worried that this case will queer your promotion."

"I don't deserve the shit, that's all I'm saying."

That may have been true, at least in a sense. Eventually, I found out that Jameson had the highest conviction rate of any homicide investigator in the state. A lot of promotions, commendations, and even a valor medal. But now, after so many years on the department, his bitterness was draining like an abscess.

"You've covered this up for three years," I pointed out. "How'd the papers get wind of these last three?"

He sputtered smoke in disgust. "One of the construction crews building the new stadium found two in one day, and one of the workmen's wives writes for *Post-Intelligencer.* So we were fucked. Then a couple days later some egghead from UW's botany department finds the third body stuffed into a hole in one of the original drain outlets to the Sound.

That fuckin' outlet had been out of service for seventy years, but this guy's in there with hipwaders collecting samples of fuckin' kelp and sea-mold. Then we were really burned. Three bodies with the same m.o., in less than a week? Next thing I know, me and the rest of my squad are getting pig-fucked by the press."

"Your compassion for the victims is heart-rending, captain," I said.

"Let me tell you something about these 'victims,'" Jameson shot back. "They're crack-whores. They're street junkies. They steal, they rip people off, they spread AIDS and other diseases. If it weren't for all this walking garbage that this candyass liberal state welcomes with open arms, then we wouldn't *have* a fuckin' drug epidemic. Shit, Health and Human Services *pays* these fuckin' people with our tax dollars! They sell their goddamn food stamps for a quarter on the dollar to buy crack. The city spends a couple hundred grand a year of our money giving these animals brand-new needles every day, and then millions more in hospital fees when they OD. Sooner or later society's gonna get fed up . . . but probably not in my fuckin' lifetime."

"That's quite a social thesis, captain. Should I start my next article with that quote?"

"Sure," he said. "But you'll have to have it transcribed."

"Transcribed?" I asked.

"They won't let you have a computer or typewriter in prison. Between the FCC violations and the tax-evasion, they'll probably give you five years, but don't worry. I'm sure they'll parole you after, say, a year and a half."

Okay, so maybe I've cut a few corners on my taxes, and I almost never use that descrambler . . . but I didn't know if he was kidding about this stuff or not. And Jameson didn't look like the kind of guy to kid about anything.

"Now that we've got that settled–come on. I need a drink."

***

Jameson wasn't kidding about that either, about needing a drink. He slammed back three beers–tall boys—in about ten minutes while I sipped a Coke. Of all places, he'd taken me to The Friendly Tavern at James Street and Yesler, what most people would call a "bum" bar. It was on the same block as the city's most notorious subsidized housing complex, a couple of liquor stores and two bail bondsman's. Right across the street was the county courthouse.

"You sure know how to pick the posh spots," I said.

"Aw, fuck all those ritzy socialist asshole pinkie-in-the-air places up town," Jameson replied. "I want to drink, I don't want to listen to some bald lesbian read poetry. I don't want to listen to a bunch of fruitcake men with fingernail polish and black lipstick talk about art. I'll tell ya, one day Russia and the Red Chinese are gonna invade us, and this'll probably be the first city they take. When they get a load of the art-fag freak show we've got going on here, they'll just say fuck it and nuke us. All this fuckin' tattoo homo goth shit, women in combat boots, guys with Kool-Aid-colored mohawks swapping tongues in public and girls sticking their hands down each other's pants while they're walking down fuckin' Fifth Avenue. Everybody wearing black, of course–'cos it's *chic,* it's *sophisticated.* Everybody with all this ridiculous metal shit in their face, fuckin' rings in their nose and lips, rivets in their tongues. Nobody gives a shit about global terrorism or the trade-deficit–all they care about is getting their dicks pierced and picking up the next Maryland Mansion album."

"I think that's *Marilyn Manson*," I said, "and, boy, you're packing a whole lot of hatred, Captain."

"I wouldn't call it hatred."

"Oh? You consider the homeless, the drug-addicted, and

destitute to be, and I quote 'walking garbage' and you've just railed against alternative lifestyles with more invective than a right-wing militia newsletter. If that's not hatred, what is it?"

"Focused animosity."

"Ah, thanks for the clarification," I said, amazed at this guy.

"The world doesn't ask much, you know? Work a job and obey the law–that's all anyone needs to do to be okay in my book." He slugged more beer, then glanced around in loathe. "The art-faggots, the dykes and the pinkos? I guess I can put up with them–most of 'em got jobs and they tend to stay out of the per-capita crime percentages. I'm just sick of seeing it, you know? Fuckin' pinkos."

"Didn't that term die out in the '70s?" I speculated. "Like when *All In The Family* went off the air?"

Jameson didn't hear me. He took another slug of beer, another loathsome glance around at the bar's patronage. "But this shit here? The rummies, the winos? They're the ones that get my goat. Ever notice how shit-hole bars like this are always full the first week of the month?"

I squinted at him. "I don't know what you're talking about."

"It's 'cos on the first of the month, they all get their three-hundred-dollar SSI checks. Then they come here and sit around like a bunch of waste-products and drink till the money's gone. Then the rest of the month they pan-handle or mug people for booze money."

I had to protest. "Come on, Captain. I read the crime indexes. Incidences of the homeless mugging citizens are almost non-existent. They pan-handle because there's nothing else they can do. And they drink because they're genetically dependent on alcohol. They can't help it."

"Gimme a break," he said. "I'm not surprised at something like that from a lib journalist. Jesus Christ. Everything's a *disease* today. If you're a lazy piece of shit, you've got *affect disorder.* If you're a fat fuck, it's an inherited *glandular imbalance.* If your kid's a wise-ass, smart-ass punk fucking up in school, it's *amotivational syndrome* or *attention-deficit disorder.* What they all really need is a good old fashioned ass-kicking. Crack 'em in the head with a two by four enough times and they'll get the message that they gotta pull their own weight in this world. And these fuckin' rummies and crackheads? Oh, boo-hoo, poor them. It's not their fault that they're dope addicts and drunks, it's this *disease* they have. It's this thing in their *genes* that makes them be useless stinking fuck-ups on two legs. Put all that liberal shit in a box and mail it to someone who cares. I'll bet you give money to the ACLU and the fuckin' Civil Liberties Union. If they had it their way, we'd all be paying sixty-percent taxes so these fucking bums could drink all day long and piss and shit in the street whenever they want."

This hypocrisy made me sick. If anyone in this bar were an alcoholic, it was Jameson. "You know something, Captain?" I said. "You're the most hateful, insensitive asshole I've ever met in my life. You're an ignorant bigot and a police-state fascist. You probably call African-Americans niggers."

"Naw, we call 'em boot-lips and porch monkeys. You don't see white people prancing down the street rubbing their fuckin' crotches and playing cop-killer rap out of those ghetto blasters, do you? I'se Amf-nee, I'se Tyrome. Kill duh poe-leece.. Kill duh poe-leece."

"I'm leaving," I said. "This is incredulous. What the hell am I doing even sitting here with you? What the hell has this got to do with your psycho killer?"

"Everything," he said, and ordered his fourth beer. "It doesn't matter what my views are–you're a journalist, you're supposed to report the truth. Even if you hate me . . . you're supposed to report the truth, right?"

"Yeah, right."

"Well none of the other papers are doing that. None of them have even queried my office to ask anything about the status of our investigation. It's easier just to write these horror-movie articles about the three poor victims who were brutally murdered by this killer, and about how the big bad police aren't doing anything about it because they don't care about street whores or the homeless. They want to make this look like Jack the fucking Ripper so they can sell more papers and have something to talk about at their pinko liberal bisexual cocktail parties."

I finished my Coke, grabbed my jacket off the next stool. "I'm out of here, Captain. You've given me no reason to stay and listen to any more of this bullshit. You want me to write a news article about police diligence regarding this case? That's a laugh. You haven't shown me anything. In fact the *only* thing you've shown me is that the captain of the homicide unit is a drunk and a bigot. And go ahead and report me to IRS and FCC. I'll take my chances."

"See? You're just like the others–you're a phony."

"Why do you say that?"

"Because you haven't even asked me the most important question. Why? Because you don't care. All you care about is putting the police on the hot-seat just like all these other non-writing chumps."

It was very difficult for me to not walk out right then. But I have to admit, I was piqued by what he'd suggested. "All right. What's the question I didn't ask?"

"Come on, you went to college, didn't you? You're a smart guy." Jameson drained half of the next beer in one chug, then lit another cigarette off the last stub. "When you've got a string of related murders, what's the first thing you've got to do?"

I shrugged. "Establish suspects?"

"Well, yeah, but before you can do that, you have to verify the common-denominators of the modus. Once you've done that, you gotta pursue a workable analysis of the of the motive. Remember, this is a *serial killer* we're talking about, not some PCP-head punk knocking over 7-Elevens. Serial killers are calculating, careful. Some guy all fucked up on ice goes out and rapes a girl—that's easy. I'll have the fucker in custody in less than forty-eight hours and I'll send him up for thirty years. But a serial killer?"

"All right, I don't know much about this kind of stuff," I admitted. "After all, this is Seattle, not Detroit."

"Good, good," he said. "So we establish the m.o., and with that we can analyze the motive. Once we've analyzed the motive, then we determine a what?"

"Uhhhh . . . ."

"A psychological profile of the killer."

"Well, that was my next guess," I said.

"Only until we've established some working psych profile can we then effectively identify suspects."

"Okay, I'm following you."

Shaking his head, he crushed the next cigarette out in an ashtray that read *Yoo-hoo, Mabel? Black Label!* along the rim. "And? From the standpoint of a journalist, the most important question in this case is . . . what?"

The last guy in the world I wanted to look stupid in front of was Jameson. I was stressed not to say the wrong thing. "Why, uh, why is the killer . . . cutting off their hands?"

"Right!" he nearly yelled and cracked his open palm against the bar-top. "Finally, one of you ink-stained liberal press schmucks has got it! The police can't do squat until they've established an index of suspects, and we can't do that until we've derived a profile of the killer. Why is he killing these girls and taking their hands?"

"But . . ." My thoughts tugged back and forth. "If he

84

cuts off their hands, they can't leave fingerprints, can't be identified, and if they can't be identified, your investigation becomes obstructed."

"No, no, no," he griped. "In my office I *showed* you the ID list. We ID'd more than half of the victims already. A lot of the girls still had their ID's on their bodies when we found them. So what's that tell you?"

"The killer doesn't—"

"Right, he either thinks he's hidden the bodies so well that they'll never be found, or he doesn't care if they're ID'd. And, from there, the most logical deduction can only be?"

"He's . . . taking their hands for some other reason?" I posed.

"See? I knew you were smarter than these other bozos." Jameson actually seemed pleased that I'd figured some of it out. "That's what we've done. We've put more man-hours into this investigation than fucking Noah put into the Arc. The killer's *collecting* their hands. And when we find the reason, we'll get our suspects. Here, take this," he said, and reached down to his floor. What he hauled up was a briefcase. It felt heavy enough to contain a couple of cinder blocks.

"What is this?" I asked.

"The entire case file."

I sat back down, put on my glasses, and opened the case. "This looks like over a thousand pages of data."

"More than that," Jameson said. "Sixteen hundred so far. You want to be an honest journalist—"

"I *am* an honest journalist," I reminded him.

"—then do your homework. Read the fucking file, read the whole thing. And when you're done, if you can honestly say that me and my men are being negligent, then tell me so . . . and I'll resign my post. Deal?"

I flipped through the fat stack of paper. It looked like a *lot* of work. I was fascinated.

"Deal," I said.

"I knew you wouldn't walk out on this." Jameson, half-drunk now, rose to his feet. "I'll talk to ya soon, pal. Oh, and the beers are on you, right?" He slapped me hard on the back and grinned. "You can write 'em off on your taxes as a research expense . . ."

Jameson was afflicted by the very thing he condemned: alcoholism. That much was clear. But in spite of his hypocrisy, I had to stick to my own guns. I'm a journalist; to be honest, I had to be objective. I had to separate Jameson's drunken hatred and bigotry from the task. Not a lot of newspaper writers do that, they jump on the easiest bandwagon–and I've done that myself–to please their editors by increasing unit sales. The Green River Killer is the best example in the Pacific Northwest . . . and it was all a sham, it was all hype. Everybody jumped on the state's favorite suspect . . . and it turned out to be the wrong guy. I knew I was better than that, so I decided that it didn't matter that Jameson was a reckless racist prick. All that mattered was the quality of the job he was doing.

And it looked like he wasn't doing half-bad.

That briefcase full of paper he gave me? He wasn't exaggerating. It was the entire investigatory file on every victim, going back for three years. Jameson and his crew had left no stone unturned, no evidential hair uncombed, and no speck of evidence unexamined. Of the victims who *had* been identified, the few who'd had traceable living relatives, Jameson had personally made the notification. Not an informal letter or a soulless phone call. The Captain himself, as the major case investigator, had traveled to locales as far of as Eugene, Oregon; Los Angeles; Spokane; and in one case, San Angelo, Texas, to notify the next of kin. All departmental expenditure invoices were included in the case file; Jameson had made these trips on his own time and at his own expense.

The evidence was another thing. Jameson had cut no slack whatsoever on pursuing even the minutiae of the crime-scene evidence. Even thoroughly decomposed and mummified victim's bodies had been analyzed to the furthest extent of forensic science. From things I'd never heard of like particulate-gas chromatographs, iodine and neohydrin fingerprint scans, atomic-force microscopy assays to simple gumshoe door-to-door canvassing. Sure, when Jameson had a load on, all of his hateful pus came pouring out, but from what I could see, when he was sober, he was a state of the art homicide investigator. The guy was doing everything in his power to solve this case. It didn't matter that he was an asshole. It didn't matter that he was a raving caustic racist. Jameson was doing it all. He was working his ass off and getting no credit at all from the local press.

Then I had to weigh my own professional values. And I had to be honest. I didn't like this guy at all, but that wasn't the point. So I told it like it was when I wrote my piece for the *Times.* I reported to the readers of the biggest newspaper in the Seattle-Metro area that Captain Jay Jameson and his veteran homicide squad were doing everything humanly possible to catch the "Handyman."

The writers for the other papers about shit when they saw the detail of my article. My article, in fact, made the others look uninformed and haphazard. It made them look like the same exploitative tabloid hacks that Jameson accused them of being. But that didn't mean I was letting Jameson off the hook. If he slacked off or screwed up in any way, I'd write about that too. I gave the guy the benefit of the doubt because he deserved it. The rest was up to him.

Another thing, though. The case file contained several hundred pages of potential psychiatric analyses. I'm not stupid but I'm also not very well-versed in psych-speak. On every profile prospectus, I saw the same name: a clinical psychiatrist in Wallingford named Henry Desmond. I needed more of a layman's synopsis of these work-ups, to make my articles more coherent to the average reader. So I made an appointment to see this guy, this Dr. Henry Desmond.

"I appreciate your seeing me on such short notice, Dr. Desmond," I said when I entered the spare but spacious office. A pencil cup on his desk read: *Thorazine (100 mgs) Have A Great Day!* On the blotter lay a comic book entitled *Dream Wolves,* with cover art depicting what appeared to be sultry half-human werewolves tearing the innards out of handsome men.

"So you're the journalist, eh?"

"Yes, sir. I've got a few questions, if you don't mind."

"My last patient claimed to be about to give birth to a litter of extraterrestrial puppies. Her question was would I prefer a male or female. So I can assure you, any questions you might have will be more than welcome considering the usual."

Extraterrestrial puppies? I wondered. I took a seat facing the broad desk. Dr. Desmond was thin, balding, with very short blonde hair around the sides of his head. The dust-gray suit he wore looked several sizes too large. In fact, he looked lost behind the huge desk. A poster to the side read: *Posey Bednets And Straitjackets. Proven To Be The Very Best Three-, Four-, And Five-point Restraints In The Industry.*

Some industry. "I've got some questions, sir, about the—"

"The so-called 'Handyman' case, yes?"

Jameson must've talked to him, but that didn't make a whole lot of sense because I never told Jameson I'd be coming to see Desmond. "That's right, sir. I'm fascinated by your clinical write-ups regarding—"

"Potential profiles of the killer?"

"Yes."

He stared at me as of chewing the inside of his lip. "What you need to understand is that I don't officially *work* for the police. I'm a private consultant."

"So it's not cool with you that I mention your name as a consultant in any future articles I may write?"

"No, please. It's not . . . *cool.*"

Great, I thought. *A cork in a bottle.*

"But I'd be pleased to answer any questions you may have on an anonymous basis. The only reason I must insist on anonymity is probably obvious."

"Uh," I said. "I'm sorry, sir, but it's not quite obvious to *me.*"

The doctor let out the faintest of snorts. "If you were consulting with the police about a serial-killer case, would you want *your name* in a newspaper that the killer himself could easily read?"

Stupid! I thought. "No, sir. Of course not. This kind of thing is new to me, so I apologize for my naivete. And I guarantee you that your name won't be mentioned."

"Good, because if it is, I'll sue you and your newspaper for multiple millions of dollars," he said through a stone cold face. "And I'll win."

I stared back, slack-jawed.

"I'm kidding! My God, can't anybody today take a joke?"

I nodded glumly after a long pause. *A funny guy. Fine. Just what I need.*

"I trust it was the good Captain Jameson who sent you?"

"No, sir, he didn't *send* me. He gave me the case file to examine, and I saw your name on the prospective profiling data, so—"

"What do you think of Captain Jameson?" Desmond asked. "He's quite a character, isn't he?"

I opened my mouth to answer, but only my lips quavered.

"Come on, son. Tell me the *truth.* I'm forbidden by law to repeat anything you say."

I guess he was right. Doctor-client privilege and all that, even though I wasn't a patient. So I said it. "I think Captain Jameson is a clinical alcoholic with enough hatred in him to burn down the city . . . But I also think he's probably a pretty effective homicide investigator."

"You're correct on both counts," Desmond acknowledged. "He's a tragic man in a tragic occupation. You'd be surprised how many of my patients are veteran police officers."

This struck me as odd. As a psychiatrist, Desmond could not legally verify that Jameson was a *patient.* And I'd never suspected that he was.

Until now, perhaps.

"Your profiles," I said to move on.

"They're not profiles, not as of yet. Think of them as *possible* profiles."

"Er, right. I've read every page of the case load compiled thus far, but I'm still a little shaky on a lot of it. These are highly clinical terms, I need layman terms."

"All right. Understood. So go on."

I must've sounded like I was babbling. "Well, er, sir, it seems that you've, uh—"

"Compartmentalized the potential clinical profiles into three groups?"

"Yes, and—"

"And you don't know what the *hell* I'm talking about."

My shoulders slumped in the chair. "You hit the nail on the head, doctor."

Dr. Desmond stroked his bare chin as if he had a goatee. "What's the first question a paramount journalist such as yourself might be inclined to ask after examining the full details of this case?"

I'd already learned this one the hard way. "Why is the killer taking the hands? It can't be to obfuscate fingerprint discovery because he's clearly demonstrated a total lack of concern as to whether or not the authorities positively identify the victims or not."

"Excellent," Desmond said.

"Which means that the killer is *collecting* the hands, for some unknown reason."

"Well, not *unknown*. There are several *suspected* reasons detailed in the case file."

I nodded. "That's what I'm not clear on, sir."

In his hand, Desmond was diddling with a small pale-blue paperweight that said *PROLIXIN — IV & IM* on it. "Consider the most obvious symbological reference. There's been no evidence of semen or prophylactic lubricant in the vaginal barrels or rectal vaults of any of the victims, which indicates a sexual dysfunction. He's picking the women up and strangling them, then he's cutting of their hands. This is a strong evidence signature; the crime describes an inner-personal pathology. So you're right. He's *collecting* their hands. Possibly as trophies. The same way Serbs severed the heads of so many Bosnians. The same way the T'u Zhus removed the penises of invaders from nearby tribes. Yes? Taking parts off the enemy. *Offending* parts."

Suddenly, I was beginning to see. "But who's the enemy in *this* case?"

"Clearly, the mother. The first profile possibility indicates someone who was severely abused as a child by the mother-figure. A woman who beat the child, with *her hands.* A woman who molested the child, with *her hands.* The mother who invaded the child's private parts—*with her hands.*"

It made some sense . . . but there were still more possibilities. "And the second profile?" I asked.

91

"The converse. The polar opposite, in a sense. No abuse in this instance but simply a *lack* of the necessary primal need to be touched—by the mother. We're talking about the sheer lack of the facilitation of the nurturing touch. All babies *need* to be touched by the mother. If they're not, the incidence of subsequent sociopathy is increased by one hundred percentage points. Put a newborn hamster in a cage by itself, and it dies in a few days. Even if it's regularly hand fed by a human. Put it in a cage with a dummy mother, and it lives but later in life it becomes violent, anti-social, homicidal. It's never *touched* by the mother. Any mammalian species that aren't nurtured by the mother never grow up right. Then put this in *human* terms. Humans—the most complex mammalian species. They bear the most vulnerable newborns, which require constant attention by the mother to survive. The mother's touch. Infants who aren't sufficiently touched by their mothers suffer numerous psychological disorders. Theodore Kaczynski, the world-famous Unabomber, never became socially adjusted in adulthood in spite of his high IQ and expert propensity for mathematics. Why? Because complications shortly after his birth required him to be incubated for several weeks—separated from his mother's nurturing touch. It's something that all babies need, and he didn't get it. Look what happened later."

The office sat just behind the McDonald's on Stone Way; all I could smell were french fries and Big Macs, which kind of threw me for a loop: smelling fast food while listening to psych profiles seemed bizarre. "Both of those descriptions make sense," I said. "But I'm wondering—just how crazy is this guy?"

"In Profile #1, the perpetrator may be quite 'crazy,' to use your term. He may be psychopathic or merely sociopathic, but more than likely the former. He's probably in the mid-or late-stages of a hallucinotic syndrome, and has long since experienced a mid-phased episodic reality break."

Christ, I thought. *You need a doctorate in psychiatry just to talk to this guy. Talking to him's worse than reading his write-ups.* "The clinical terms are way over my head, Dr. Desmond," I admitted. "If you could dumb this down a little?"

"Clinically, we would call Profile #1 a graduated bipolar symbolist. The effect of his illness has a tendency to switch off and on at times relative to his delusion, and to put it in general terms, when he's *off,* he's able to function normally in society, but when he's *on,* he is indeed 'crazy.' He becomes overwhelmed by some facet of his delusional fixation to the extent that he hallucinates. The women he murders are symbols. He *sees* his victims as his mother, as the self same person who so heinously abused him as a child."

"Jeeze, that sounds pretty serious."

"Well, it is given the gravity of the crimes. It's unusual, though, that someone could maintain this level of bipolarity for three years. If there's anything 'promising' about the diagnosis, it is the graduated aspect. He's gradually becoming more and more insane; eventually—soon, I would say—he'll lose his ability to maintain social functionality. And he'll get caught rather quickly."

Promising? I thought. *Odd choice of words, but then he's the shrink.* "What about Profile #2?"

"More complicated, and less predictable," Desmond began. "Profile #2 is functionally similar in that the killer is suffering from a symbolic bipolar personality disorder. But he's not experiencing any manner of hallucinosis and his delusions are conscious and quite controllable. The fantasy element takes over. It's probably quite like a dream. When he's murdering these women—and severing their hands—he's immersed so deeply in the delusion that he's probably not even consciously aware of what he's doing. It's a fixation disorder that's run amok. Am I losing you?"

"Well, a little, yes." *A little, my ass.*

"He's dreaming of something he never had. Only, regrettably, he's acting out the dream in real life. Is that synopsis *cool* with you, young man?"

But I still didn't get it. "A dream . . . of cutting off hands?"

"No, no. Be intuitive. The perpetrator doesn't see it that way. He sees it as claiming what he never had as a child. Remember–the facilitation of the mother's nurturing touch. All infants need to be touched; the perpetrator was not. That should answer your question about what exactly he's *doing* with the hands."

I stared at him, gulped. And the implication was disgusting. "You mean he's . . . taking the hands—"

"He's taking the hands home," Desmond finished, "and putting them on his body. His mother is at last touching him. Nurturing him. But now, in adulthood, the delusion is so thoroughly contorted and transfigured—he's probably masturbating with the hands too."

What a screwed up world, with screwed up people. "Christ," I said. "That's . . . sick."

"But so is our perpetrator," Desmond added. "There's quite a bit in our world that's sick, twisted, wrong. And quite a few people in it who don't see it that way."

"But the third," I said, "the third profile." I put my glasses on and looked back at the marked pages of the case file. "You called it a 'fixated erotomanic impulse'. What's that mean?"

Desmond's pate glimmered in a sun-break through the window. He shrugged his shoulders. "It means that in the case of this third potential profile, the killer is simply a sociopath with a hand fetish."

Simply a sociopath with a hand fetish, I thought. The terms just rolled off this guy's lips like me talking about baseball.

"It's the most remote possibility but also the worst as far as apprehension is concerned."

"Why's that?" I asked.

"It's remote because sociopaths rarely engage in mutilation crimes. But they're infinitely harder to apprehend because sociopaths, as a rule, aren't insane; therefore they're less likely to make a mistake that could lead to arrest. Sociopaths are skilled liars. They've had their whole lives to practice. Their amorality isn't a result of mental defectivity. They know what's right and what's wrong, but they choose wrong because it suits them."

They choose wrong, I thought. But Desmond had said this profile was the least likely. "If you had to make a choice yourself," I asked him, "which of the three would you put your money on?"

Desmond tsk'd, smiled a thin smile. "Abnormal psychiatry isn't an objective checklist. Profile indexes exist only through the documentation of known information. So it stands to reason that there's quite a bit out there that we *don't* know yet. It would be of little value for me to make a guess. All I can say is it's probably one of the three. But you should also consider a sexual detail that should also be obvious."

Dumb again. Dumb me. "And that would be?"

"The absence of evidence of rape. No semen in any orifice, no evidence of sexual penetration. Considering any of my three profiles, the possibility should properly be addressed that the killer is at the very least unable to achieve erection in the presence of a woman, or he may be sexually incompetent altogether."

"This is a lot of data you've given me, sir, and I'm grateful," I said, pushing my glasses up the bridge of my nose. The insights he'd given me would make for a great, comprehensive series of articles on the killer. "I really appreciate your time."

"My pleasure, young man."

I grabbed my stuff to leave, but then he held up a finger to stop me.

"One last point, though," he said. "In the cases of Profiles #1 and #2, there's a considerable formative likelihood that the killer's mother was either a prostitute, a drug addict, or both."

"That'll help my article too. Maybe if the killer reads it, it'll scare him into making a mistake, or stopping."

Desmond creaked back in his padded chair. I'm not sure if he was smiling or not, just nodding with his eyes thinned and his lips pressed together. "Perhaps it will," he said so softly it sounded like a flutter.

"Thank you," I said. But then something caught me—two things, actually, both at the same time. Behind Desmond's head, the late-afternoon sun burned, an inferno. And then my eyes flicked down to the doctor's desk blotter.

It was one of those calendar blotters, each top sheet a different month. The Tuesday and Thursday boxes for all four weeks had this written in them:

J.J. - 1:30 P.M.

J.J., I thought.

Captain Jay Jameson.

That's when I knew Jameson was it. It hit me in the head like someone dropping a flowerpot from a high window. There were still a few holes, sure. But it was one of those things where you just *knew.* It was a presage. It was something psychic.

I just knew.

I knew I had to go see him. I knew I had to get him out. But before I could even make a plan, Jameson walks right into my cubicle the next day.

"There he is. The lib journalist."

I glanced up from my copy, stared at him.

"Hey, I'm just joking," he said. "Lighten up, you'll live longer."

"You come here to bust me for my descrambler."

"What's a descrambler?" he said. "And tax evasion? Never heard of it."

"Why are you here, Captain? You want to square up with me? Those four Old English tallboys cost me $3.50 a pop. Us lib journalists don't make much."

"Good," he said. He rubbed his hands together. He grinned through that weird lined, tanned face, the shock of blond-gray hair hanging over one eye. "Let me make it up to ya. Dinner at my place. You ever had broiled langoustes with scallop mousse? My wife makes it better than any restaurant in the city. Come on."

This was a great opportunity but . . . "I've got a deadline. I'm a crime writer, remember? I'll be here at least two more hours writing up the robbery at the Ballard Safeway. My boss won't let me out of here til it's done."

Jameson jerked a gaze into the outer office. "That's your boss there, right? The fat guy in suspenders with the mole on his neck bigger than a bottlecap? I already talked to him. Safeway can wait. You're off early today, boy."

"What are you talk—"

Jameson lit a cigarette, then tapped an ash on my floor. "Your boss has sixteen parking tickets he thought his brother in the public safety building buried. I showed him the print-out from the city police mainframe."

That'll do it. I looked through the door at my boss, and all he did was frown and flick his wrist.

"All right," I said. "I guess Safeway can wait."

"Honey? This is my good friend Matt Hauge," Jameson introduced. "This is my wife, Jeanna."

I cringed when he said *good friend,* but I also knew I had to play along now. "Pleased to meet you, Mrs. Jameson," I said and shook her hand. She looked about mid-forties but well tended. Bright blond hair, good figure, probably a knockout in her younger days. *What's a good-looking woman like this doing with a busted racist drunk like Jameson?* I wondered. They didn't fit together at all. They both looked out of place standing there together. A shining figurine and a rubber dog turd.

He'd driven me from the paper to his Belltown condominium. Nice place, clean, well appointed, which didn't look right either. It was easier to picture Jameson living in an unkempt dump with smoke-stained walls, dirty dishes in the sink, and cigarette burns in a carpet that hadn't been vacuumed in years.

"Hi," she said with kind of a wan smile. "Jay hasn't stopped talking about you."

"Oh, really?" I replied.

"Oh, God, since your article in the *Times* came out, he's been like a kid at Christmas."

So that's what this was all about. The red carpet treatment. Jameson's ego and pride wouldn't let him say it, so he let his wife do it. This was his way of thanking me for giving him a good shake in print. *Or maybe it's just his way of continuing the bribe,* I considered.

"From what I can see, Mrs. Jameson, your husband's doing a top-notch job in investigating this case," I told her. "The other writers in this city have chosen not to acknowledge this—and that's wrong. I'm not doing your husband any favors here; I'm just writing it the way I see it."

"Well," she went on, "we're really grateful to you."

"No need to be, ma'am. Because if your husband drops the ball now . . . I'm going to write about that too." Then I shot Jameson a cocked grin.

"I don't *drop* the ball," Jameson told me and immediately lit a cigarette. "Don't believe me? Check my performance ratings."

"I already have," I said. "And you're right." Then I glanced over at the tv in the corner. "Say, is that a descrambler you've got there?"

"Funny guy. I like a lib journalist with a sense of humor," he said, slapping me hard on the back and showing me into the dining room. Warm, exotic aromas swam around the room. "What would you like to drink?" Jameson's wife asked.

"A Coke would be fine."

Another hard slap to the back. It was getting old. "Come on, have a drink," Jameson insisted. "You're off duty."

"Maybe later," I said, half lost of breath.

"Dinner'll be right up," Jeanne said, then disappeared into the aromatic kitchen.

Jameson and I sat down at the table simultaneously. I knew I had him pegged, but I also knew I still needed more. This was the big league. He was a decorated city detective, I was just a reporter.

"Look, man," he said. "I ain't too good at, you know—expressing gratitude? But your article really helped me out . Not just me but my whole squad. So . . . thanks."

"Don't thank me yet," I said. "Like I just got done telling your wife, you step on your dick, I'm gonna write about that too."

"I hear ya—"

"And it's not just one article, you know. I'm writing a *series* of related articles about the killer," I informed him.

"Oh, yeah?"

"Yeah. This isn't just some fly-by-night crime piece. It's a comprehensive serial-killer story. People want to know, so I'm gonna tell them." It was time to play the card. "I've already talked to Dr. Desmond, and he gave me a lot of clinical info on the case. It'll be a highly informative series."

Jameson's jaw dropped so hard I thought his lower lip

would slap the dining room table. "You-you-you've talked to Dr. Desmond?"

"Yeah, sure. I saw his name on those profile write-ups you gave me. My next article's going to detail his first profile: the killers who's cutting off his victim's hand out of a symbolic and hallucinatory act of revenge. Then I'll write another about the second profile: the homicidal fantasist whose talking the hands to facilitate what he never got as a child. The nurturing touch of the mother." I paused for a moment, just to gauge his reaction.

All he did was look at me *real* funny.

"Yeah, he gave me all kinds of insights for my series," I added. "It could get national notice."

"Uh, yeah, sure," Jameson said. Was he faltering? Did I throw him a hard slider? "Desmond's an odd cookie, and talk about ego? Shit. He can barely walk into a room 'cos his head's so big. But he does know his shit. That guy can slap a profile faster than the president can whip it out."

"I wouldn't put it in quite those terms, Captain," I said, "but Dr. Desmond does seem to be a qualified expert."

Jeanne brought out the drinks, then smiled bashfully, and said, "It'll be just another minute."

I nodded as she scurried back to the kitchen. "So what are we having?" I asked Jameson. "Linguini and something?"

"Langoustes. Petite lobster tails from Britain. Flash-broiled in garlic and lime butter and topped with scallop mousse." Jameson half drained a can of Rainier Ice. "I hope you're hungry."

"I'm starving. Missed lunch."

"Oh, yeah. Bet'cha hate it when you have to put in ten hours."

"Ten? Are you kidding me. Ten's an easy day."

Each time Jameson dragged on his cigarette, I watched a third of it burn down; then he'd light another. "Look, I'm sorry about all that shit I said a few days ago. I didn't mean

it—it wasn't me. I was just having a bad day, you know?"
He grinned. "Even racist police-state cops have bad days."

"Thank God I never pulled up my sleeve. Then you
would've seen my Maryland Mansion tattoo."

"Oh, you've got one too?" Jameson exploded laughter, a
bit too loudly.

Dinner was served, and I have to admit, I've probably
never had a better seafood meal in my life. The scallop
mousse melted in my mouth, and those langouste things
tasted better than any lobster I've ever had. During the meal,
we tried to talk openly, but Jameson—the more he drank—
dominated the conversation with cop talk. After a while,
I could see that his wife was getting uncomfortable, even
embarrassed, and after a little more time, she just gave up. I
felt sorry for her.

"So we're all standing around the morgue slab with the
M.E.!" Jameson bellowed after his fifth beer, "and the corpse
cracks a fart! I kid you not!"

Yeah, I felt *really* sorry for her.

"So then Dignazio says, 'Damn, he must get his chili
dogs at Schultze's 'cos that fart smells just like mine!'"

The poor woman just wilted where she sat.

"This was a fantastic meal, Mrs. Jameson. Thanks very
much," I said. "But I guess I better get going now."

"Bullshit!" Jameson said. Then he put his arm around me
and shook me, all the while looking at his wife. "Honey,"
he said. "I gotta take this boy out for a nightcap, all right? I
gotta teach this man to drink!"

"No, really—" I started.

"Come on, don't be a candyass!"

"Just be careful," Mrs. Jameson said.

I'm no big drinker but I still had a few things to snuff
out. Bar-hopping with Jameson would provide the perfect
opportunity.

We got up to leave. That's when I noticed two of the framed pictures along the fireplace mantle; there were just a few.

I put my glasses on and looked.

A wedding picture of a much younger Jameson and his wife. Some snapshots of old people: relatives, I presumed. Aunts and uncle, grandparents, the like. A freeze-frame of a beautiful cheerleader wagging pom-poms and doing a split—it was obviously Jameson's wife back in high school days. Then—

A framed picture of a dark-haired adult with his arm around a cock-eyed kid with a bad haircut.

Jameson, I thought. *The kid's Jameson . . .*

"No kids yet, I see," I said and took my glasses off. I suspected this might be dangerous ground but I had to go for it.

"No," Mrs. Jameson peeped.

"Not yet," Jameson piped in. "We're still waiting for the right time."

Man, you're fifty and she's gotta be forty-five, I thought. *Better not wait much longer.*

Jameson jangled his keys. "Come on, lib. Let's go have some fun."

I turned to his wife. "Mrs. Jameson. Thanks very much for the excellent meal. You could get a job at any restaurant in town; you'd blow all of those master chefs out of the water."

The woman blushed. "Thank you. Come by again soon."

"Later, babe," Jameson bid and yanked me out of there. He guffawed all the way down the stairs to the parking garage.

"So where you wanna go?" he asked. "A strip joint?"

"And all this time I thought you were gonna take me to hear bald lesbians read poetry," I joked.

"Aw, fuck that shit," he answered, beer fumes wafting out of his mouth. "Let's see some *meat.*"

"Pardon me if I'm misinformed, Captain, but there really aren't any strip joints in Seattle. The girls all gotta wear bikinis via county code, and the only thing you can drink there is orange juice or sodas."

Another loud guffaw. "Pal, you don't know the strip joint I know!"

I'm sure I don't, I thought. When we'd just stepped into the elevator into the parking garage, I slapped my breast pocket. "Oh, shit."

"What's wrong? You just shit your pants?"

"I left my glasses in your condo," I admitted.

"Well go on back up and get them and I'll get the car." He elbowed me. "And no funny business with the wife . . . or I'll have ta kill you."

He burst more laughter as I jogged back up the stairs.

"I'm sorry," I said to Mrs. Jameson when she answered my knock. "I left my glasses here."

"Oh, come in," she said. I could smell from her breath that she'd already had a stiff one since we'd left. "Where would they be?"

"The table, or maybe the mantle when I was looking at the pictures," I said.

I scanned the table—nothing.

"Here they are," she said, picking them up off the mantle.

"Thanks."

"I apologize for the way Jay gets sometimes," the words stumbled from her mouth. "He has a little too much to drink, and . . . well, you know."

You ain't kidding I know, I thought.

"But you should also know that your article really pumped him up," she went on. "I haven't seen him happy in years, but your article really made him happy. He's worked hard for so long. It's wonderful to see someone give him recognition in the press."

I shrugged. "He's doing a good job on the case. That's why I wrote the piece."

"Well, anyway, thank you," she said.

The look she gave me then? Christ. She brought her arms together in front, pressed her breasts together. Her nipples stuck through her blouse like golf cleats. *Fuck,* I thought. *Is she offering herself to me . . . for the article?*

"If you don't mind my asking," I changed the subject. "What's this picture here?" I pointed to the man with his arm around the boy. "Is that your husband, the child?"

"Yes that's him with his father," she told me. "Jay was seven. His father was killed a few weeks after that picture was taken."

"Oh . . . I'm sorry." My eyes scanned the photos. "Where's his mother?"

"Jay never knew his mother," she said. "She ran out the day he was born."

The facilitation of the mother's nurturing touch, I thought as Jameson squealed his Grand Am out of the parking garage. Everything I'd observed so far backed up everything Desmond had told me . . .

"So how'd you like the grub? Better than the cafeteria at the *Times?*"

"It was fantastic. Your wife is one dynamite cook."

"Yeah, she's a good kid," he said. "She's hung with me through thick and thin, and believe me, there's been a lot of thin. Too bad I can't do more for her."

"What do you mean?"

He steered down Third Avenue. "It didn't help when you brought up kids. Last couple of years, it's been like playing pool with a piece of string."

"Sorry," I said.

"But that's my problem, not yours," he perked up. "Let's go have some fun!"

We rode a ways. The streetlights shimmered as the warm air roved down the avenue. We stopped at a red light at third and Marion, and several homeless people approached the car.

"Shine your windshield for a buck, mister," a decrepit man said.

"Get the *fuck* away from the car!" Jameson yelled. "I just had it washed!"

"Hey, mister, relax. We was just askin'."

A woman in rotten clothes approached the other side of the car. Toothless, Staggering.

"Tell that junkie bum bitch to get away from my car!" Jameson yelled.

Then he yanked his gun out of his shoulder holster.

"Are you nuts!" I shouted at him.

The two vagrants scampered off, terrified.

"Yeah, you *better* get out of here, you pieces of shit!" Jameson yelled. "Christ, you people smell worse than the bottom of a fuckin' dumpster!"

"What the hell is wrong with you, man?" I said. "You can't be pulling your gun on people for shit like that."

Jameson reholstered his pistol, chuckling. "Cool off. I just wanted to put a scare in 'em. Bet they shit their pants, huh? See, I just saved the city a clean-up fee. Usually they shit in the street."

"They're homeless, for God's sake. They got nothing."

"Fuck that pinko shit," he said, then bulled through the red light.

It occurred to me then that Jameson had a harder load on than I thought. "Hey, look, Captain. You're pretty lit. Why don't you let me drive? You're gonna get pulled over at this rate."

Jameson laughed. "Any cop in this city pulls *me* over, he's transferred to the impound lot in the morning. What's up your ass?"

"Nothing," I said. I knew I had to grin and bear it. But I still had a few more questions to ask. *Just be careful,* I told myself. "Fuckin' junkies, fuckin' bums." Jameson's eyes remained dead on the street. "Everybody asking for a handout. I never asked for no handouts."

"Some people are more fortunate than others," I said.

"Oh, don't give me that liberal pantywaist *bullshit,*" he spat, spittle flecking the inside of the windshield. "I never had nothing. My father died when I was seven, died in a fuckin' steel mill when an ingot fell on him off a lift-clip. After that I got hocked into the fuckin' foster care system. So I don't want to hear no shit about poor people from poor environments. I got out of that hellhole, graduated high school, got my degree, and now I'm running the fuckin' homicide squad in one of the biggest cities on the west coast."

But I was still remembering what his wife had said. "What, uh, what about your mother?" I asked.

Jameson lead-footed it through another red light. "My mother? Fuck her." Beer fumes filled the car. "My mother beat feet the same day she dropped me. That dirty bitch wasn't nothing but a junkie whore. She was street-shit. She was walking garbage just like that whore just tried to smudge up my windshield. Far as I'm concerned–I never had a mother . . ."

It got to the point where almost anything Jameson did or said would support some facet of Dr. Desmond's profile. A prostitute for a mother, who abandoned him at birth. No nurturing touches as an infant, no mother-figure in the formative years. An ability to control his symbolic delusion to the extent that he can function in society and maintain steady employment. A man who is probably married but probably doesn't have children. A man with a mounting inability to perform sexually.

I also found it interesting that Jameson's favorite places to drink were bars in the derelict districts, bars in which any of the sixteen previous victims might easily have hung out. I wondered what Dr. Desmond would think about that?

Oh yeah, I knew he was the one. But what was I going to do about it?

The next couple of hours were pretty paralyzing. Jameson dragged me around to three more dive bars, getting drunker in each one, his hatred boiling. Loud, obnoxious, belligerent. At one point I thought one of the barkeeps was going to throw him out, but I prayed that wouldn't happen. Knowing Jameson—and as drunk as he was—he'd probably yank out his gun, might shoot someone. But before that could happen, I got him out of there.

Then the end came pretty fast after that.

"I'm a crime reporter for the *Times.*" I flashed my press ID to the two doctors in the ER. "Earlier tonight, I was with Captain Jay Jameson of the city police homicide unit—"

One of the doctors, a balding guy with long hair, squinted over at me from a scrub sink. "You know that guy?" The doctor's nametag read Parker.

"That's right. I was drinking with him in some area bars," I admitted. "When his name was logged in as an in-patient, the night-editor at my paper contacted me."

"Fuck, the guy was drinking," another doctor said. This one was big, with a trimmed beard; his nametag read MOLER. He was taking instruments out of an autoclave. "No wonder his blood was so thin. He damn near bled to death right in front of us. He took three pints before we could stabilize him. What happened?"

"I was dragging him out of a bar about two hours ago," I told them. "He was pretty drunk. I was about to put him in the car when he bolted. The guy just ran off across Jackson and disappeared under the overpass. I couldn't find him. The biggest reason for my concern is Captain Jameson said some things to me tonight that lead me to believe he may be—"

"This psycho who's been killing girls and cutting off their hands," Parker finished.

I stared at them, slack-jawed. "How–how did you know?"

Dr. Moler snickered. "When the EMTs brought him in, he had a severed hand in his pants."

"Jesus," I muttered. "What happened to him?"

"Looks like after he ran off from you," Parker explained, "he must've picked up a hooker, then he made his move, but she shot him. He was lying in the middle of Jackson when the EMTs found him. But it must've been his second girl of the night 'cos he already had one hand on him."

"Shit," I said. "I called the cops the minute he bolted, told them my suspicions, but they didn't take me serious."

"We'll show 'em the hand we found in his pants," Moler said. "*Then* they'll take you serious."

"So you said his condition is stable?" I asked.

"We stabilized the blood loss and ligged an artery. But the x-rays showed a cranial fracture—hematoma. He's prepped for more surgery but I wouldn't give him more than one chance in ten of making it."

"Where is he now?" I asked. "I really need to talk to him."

Parker pointed across the ER. "He's in the ICU prep cove. Second floor'll be down to take him up in a few minutes. You want to go see him, go ahead. But don't hold your breath on him regaining consciousness."

"Thanks," I said, and at the same moment several paramedics burst through the ER doors with what looked like a burn victim on a gurney. "Great!" Parker yelled. "My relief's two hours late, and now I got a spatula special!"

I rushed to the prep cove and there he was: Jameson.

Tubes down his throat, tubes up his nose, strapped to a railed bed. An IV line ran from a bag of saline to his arm. He looked dead.

"Hey, hey," I said. I patted his face. "I guess you're in a coma, huh, Captain? Well you know what? They got you for the whole thing now. I knew you were the one."

His slack, lined face just lay there like a bad wax mask. "Once Dr. Desmond finds out the details, he'll realize that his profile fits you to a tee. He's a smart man. He'll back up my allegation one-hundred percent."

I patted his face a few more times. No response.

Then I took the needle-cover off the hypodermic I'd brought along. "Yeah, I knew you were the one. I knew you were the perfect dupe to take the fall." The hypo was full of potassium dichlorate. It'd kill him in minutes and wouldn't show up on a tox screen. I injected the whole thing into his IV connector.

Then Jameson's eyes slitted open.

"You're a pretty damn good cop, Captain," I gave him. "You got any idea how hard I worked burying those bodies over the last three years? And there are twenty-one, by the way, not sixteen. You did a great job of keeping 'em out of the papers . . . until those last three. Just dumb luck for me, huh?"

He began to quiver on the bed, veins throbbing at his temples.

I leaned down close to his ear, whispered. "But that really screwed up my game when the victims started making the press. I thought I was gonna have to lay low now, get the junkie bitches from out of town. But you solved all that for me."

I grinned down at him. His eyes opened a little more, to stare at me.

"Yeah, I knew you were the one, all right. The minute

Desmond explained those profiles to me, and when I saw that picture of you with your father. No mother, just a father who died the same year. And, Christ, man! You were Desmond's patient! The press'll eat that up! Homicide cop seeing a shrink–homicide cop turns out to be the killer. It's great, isn't it? It's perfect!"

See, after I dragged him out of that last bum bar, I shoved him in the passenger seat of his car. The drunk bastard had already passed out. I drove down Jackson when there was no traffic, cracked him hard in the head with the butt of my own piece, then shot him in the groin. I was aiming for the femoral artery, and I guess I did a damn good job of hitting it. He bled all over the place; I knew the fucker was going to kick.

Then I stuck the hand in his pants and shoved him out of the car.

The whole thing worked pretty well, I'd say.

"Don't die on me yet, asshole," I whispered, pinching his cheeks. "See, Desmond had it right with his profiles. Only it turns out the real killer was the least likely of the bunch–just a sociopath with a hand fetish."

It was hard not to laugh right in his face.

Jameson's hand raised an inch, then dropped. He was tipping out but I gotta give the old fucker credit. He managed to croak out a few words.

"They'll never believe it," he said.

"Oh, they'll believe it," I assured him. "What? You're gonna tell them what *really* happened? Not likely. In two minutes you'll be dead from cardiac arrest."

"Lib motherfucker," he croaked. "Pinko piece'a shit . . ."

"That's the spirit!" I whispered. "Go out kicking! But—"

His eyelids started drooping again. This was it.

"Not yet! Don't die yet," I said, squeezing his face. "There's still one more thing I haven't told you, and it's something you gotta know."

Spittle bubbled from his lips. I could see him struggling to keep his eyes open, fighting to keep conscious just a few more seconds.

"Remember when I went back up to your condo to get my glasses?" I said. "What do you think I did to your wife, dickbrain? That hand they found in your pants? It was your *wife's* right hand!"

Jameson tremored against his restraints. He shook and shook, like someone had just stuck a hot wire in him. Down the hall, I could hear the elevator opening, the crash team coming to take him up to surgery. *Don't bother, guys,* I thought.

But just before Jameson died, I managed to tell him the final detail. "That's right, I stuck her right hand in *your* pants, Captain. And her *left* hand? I got it safe, right here with me."

Then I patted my crotch and grinned.

They took him up, and his obit ran the next day . . . along with everything else. Homicide captain investigating the Handyman Case, found with his own murdered wife's hand in his pants? The same shrink he was seeing for alcoholism and sexual dysfunction corroborating that Jameson fit the profile?

Case closed.

And don't forget what Desmond said about sociopaths. They're skilled liars. They've had their whole lives to practice. They know what's right and what's wrong, but they choose wrong because it suits them.

That sounds good to me.

I'll just have to bury the next bodies deeper.

THE TABLE

Her name was Elaine. Some uncanny static seemed to lift several strands of her hair off her shoulders; they hung there like sun-colored threads in basements murk. Graham suspected it must be her just-as-uncanny excitement.

About the table.

He drained the last of his beer, set the bottle down on an ancient steamer trunk that was next to an ancient Philco record-changer cabinet. What a strange place; the owner had died within the past few days, and he'd been a junk collector.

But Graham got back to the point. "Your fascination with the table . . . It's intriguing."

"I'm a kink," Elaine giggled. It was a sultry giggle, and it suited the rest of her. "What can I say? That's why my last boyfriend dumped me–said I was too *perverted* for him. Can you *imagine?* A *guy* saying that?"

To her? Graham could. After their conversation at the Crossroads–a proverbial redneck dump full of redneck tramps—Elaine effervesced, in spite of her earthy language and peculiarities.

"So where's this autopsy table?" he asked instead of answering her question.

"Not an autopsy table, a dissection table," she corrected, and already her erecting nipples were betraying her excitement. "Place just outside of town, Wroxeter. It used to be an abbey, but they closed that down–then the state reopened it because they needed an annex lab for the university medical school. Couple years ago–"

She left the story dangling, half-finished, her attentions diverted as she drifted more than walked toward the dusty metal table in the corner. Large rust-like stains sullied the surface. Dried blood. Nobody had cleaned it, which seemed odd. "Old Man Halm bought it from the police auction, and put it down here with all his other junk. He's the town eccentric, collects junk that has a history."

Graham watched her from behind: moonlight from the small eye-level window silhouetted her curvaceousness– an enticing black cutout. She had her hand on the table, touching its metal as though it were iconic, or resonant with some cryptic magic.

"The old man bought it from a *police auction?*" Graham asked confoundedly.

"Well, sure. After it happened, the police took the table out of the school and impounded it as evidence. But there were no fingerprints on it so they eventually put it up with for auction. They do an auction every year, but it's mostly drug-dealers' cars and stuff bought with drug money that the cops confiscate during raids. I guess they figured the school would re-buy it, but Halm got there first. He told them not to even bother cleaning it–the whacko."

Sounds to me like YOU'RE the whacko, Elaine, Graham thought and smiled to himself. "And?"

She didn't hear him. She was staring at the table, tracing her finger up and down its run-off gutter, around its drain. She let out a long hot breath. Graham wasn't sure but he thought she was rubbing the finger of her other hand up and down over the crotch of her cut-off jeans. From behind, her calves and thighs seemed to tense.

Yeah, she's a whacko, all right. The table was turning her on the way a Chippendale dancer might turn on a normal woman.

Graham cleared his throat, to nudge her back. "Are you keeping me in suspense on purpose? What's the rest of the story on the table, Elaine?"

"Oh, oh," she mumbled, coming out of her demented muse. "Sorry, I—" The hands of her luscious silhouette fell to her sides; the coltish legs untensed. "Somebody abducted one of the female med students. He raped her, murdered her, then dissected her."

"And that . . . *What?* It—"

"It turns me on." Her voice lowered, grew husky in its heat. "It drives me crazy. I'm one of those girls you read about, or see on Springer. I write to serial-killers on death row, I collect murderer memorabilia, I've been to Ed Gein's grave and Jeffrey Dahmer's apartment building. I even bought a sketch on eBay by John Wayne Gacy." She shrugged in plain honestly. "It's my fetish—this sort of thing. It's a–shit, I even used to be a psych major. There's a term for it." The moon-tinged darkness seemed alive with her breath. "An erotopathic totem," she remembered through her lust. "A physical object that activates an aberrant sexual compulsion."

Graham was speechless.

Her shoulders slumped. "I'm making this easy for you. Most guys can't handle a girl who's into this. You can walk out right now, and I'll understand."

"Am I walking out?"

Graham remained standing, facing her silhouette. Now the hot breath was a hot sigh of relief. The next gesture would've been trashy were it anyone else, but for her—when she slipped out of the halter and shorts—it seemed a flawless aspect of the dynamic, an integration of the moment. As she stripped, she continued calmly, "So what's your story, Graham? You wanted to get laid so you walked into the bar and saw me?"

"It wasn't exactly in that order," he replied. "I walked into the bar, I saw you, and now . . ."

She smiled in the dark. She sat up on the table. The giggle again, then she said, "And you sure as shit know my story. I know I don't have to say it but I want to anyway because it would turn me on even more."

"Say it," Graham told her.

"I want you to fuck me on this table. I want you to fuck me on the same exact table that that girl was raped and murdered and dissected on—"

"It wasn't exactly in that order," he repeated. Graham was strong. She was not. He'd quickly extracted the plastic bag from his back pocket, withdrew the diethyl-ether-drenched rag, and clamped it over her face.

"No," he whispered again, just a few moments before she would lose consciousness. He wanted her to hear it. "Not exactly in that order."

Then he was reaching into his other pocket, for his little case of scalpels.

DEATH, SHE SAID

"Life," I said.

I'd said it to myself, to my reflection in the rearview as I peeled the cardboard cover off the razor blade. Yeah, life.

I was all set; I was going to kill myself. Oh, I know what you're thinking. Sure, fella. All the time you're hearing about how suicidal tendencies are really just pleas for attention, cries for help. Fuck that. I didn't want help. I wanted to die.

I had one of those Red Devil brand blades, the kind you cut carpet with, or scrape paint off windows. Real sharp. I'd read somewhere that if you do it laterally, you bleed to death before the blood can clot. I sure as shit didn't want to pull a stunt like that and blow it. I could picture myself sitting in some psyche ward with bandaged wrists—a perfect ass. I wanted to do it right.

Why? Long story. I'll give you the abridged version.

I'd spent my whole life trying to make something good for myself, or maybe I should say what I *thought* was good turned out to be nothing. It was all gone in less time than it takes you to blow your nose. We had two kids. One ran off with some holistic cult, haven't seen him in a decade. The younger one died a couple weeks after her senior prom. "Axial metastatic mass," the neurologist called it. A fuckin' brain tumor is what I called it. Worst part was I never really knew them. It was my wife who brought them up, carried the load. I was too busy putting in 12, 14 hours a day at the firm, like airline trademark infringements were more important than raising my own kids. But I still had my wife, her love, her faith in me. She was behind me every step of the way, a real gem. She quit college to wait tables so I could go to law school, gave away her own future for me. She was always there—you know what I mean? We were going to get the house painted. She went out one day to check out some colors—I was too busy suing some company that made bearings for airplane wheels—but she never made it home. Drunk driver. I still had my job, though, right? Wrong. Month ago I was a senior partner in the number three firm in the country. A couple of associates decided it might be neat to bribe some jurors on a big air-wreck case I was litigating. They get disbarred, but I get blackballed. Right now I couldn't get a job jacking fries at Roy Fucking Rogers my name stinks so bad. So I guess that wraps in up nice and neat. I'm a 48-year-old attorney with no job, no family, no life.

There.

I didn't want anyone saving me, calling the paramedics or anything like that. I decided I'd do it in my car. The repo people were already after it, so I figured let 'em have it with my blood all over the suede-leather seats. I backed into an alley off the porn block. Rats, oblivious to the cold, were hopping in and out of garbage cans. Lights from an adult bookstore blinked in my face. Up ahead, I could see the hookers traipsing back and forth on L Street. They were like the rats; they didn't feel the cold. You should've seen some of the wild shit they were wearing. Leopard-skin leotards, sheer low-cut evening dresses, shorts that looked like tin foil. It was kind of funny, that my last vision in life would be this prancing tribe of whores. I had the razorblade between my fingers, poised. Each time I got ready to drag it from the

117

inside of my elbow to my wrist, I kept looking up. I wasn't chickening out, I just felt distracted. But distracted by what?

That's when I saw her, in that last half-moment before I was going to actually do it.

She'd probably been standing on the corner the whole time, I just hadn't noticed. It was like she was part of the wall, or even part of the city—darkness blended into brick.

She was staring right at me.

I stared back. She stood tall in a shiny black waistcoat whose hem came up to mid-thigh. Long legs, black stockings, high heels, I sensed she wasn't young—like the streetwalkers—yet she seemed more comely than old: graceful, beautiful in wisdom. Somehow I knew she couldn't be a hooker; looking at her, I thought of vanquished regalities—an exiled queen. She had her hands in her pockets, and she was staring.

Go away, I thought. *Can't you see I'm trying to kill myself?*

I blinked.

Then she was walking toward the car.

I stashed the razor blade under the seat. It didn't make sense. Even if she was a prostitute, no prostitute would approach a barely visible car in an alley. Maybe she'd think I was a cop. I could give her the brush-off and get back to business.

Her high heels ticked down the alley. Was she smiling? I couldn't tell. The rats scurried away.

She stopped beside the driver's window.

"I'm not sportin', I'm not datin', and I'm not looking for someone to tickle my stick," I said. "Buzz off."

Her voice was weird, like a wisp of breeze, or two pieces of silk brushing together. So soft it almost wasn't there. "Providence is a mysterious thing," she said. "It can be very nourishing."

I squinted. She was standing right there, but I couldn't see her, not really. Just snatches of her, like my eyes were a movie camera and the cameraman was drunk. All I could say in response was, "What?"

"Think before you act," she said. "There are truths you haven't seen. Wouldn't it be regrettable to die without ever knowing what they are?"

She couldn't possibly have seen what I was trying to do in the car; it was too dark, and she'd been too far away. Besides, the razor blade was under the seat.

"I can show you providence," she said. "I can show you truth."

"Oh, yeah?" I challenged. "What the fuck do you know about truth?"

"More than you think," she said.

I looked at her, still only able to see her in pieces, like slivers. I sensed more than saw. I sensed beauty in her age, not haggardness. I sensed gracility, wisdom . . .

"Come with me," she bid. "I'll show you."

I got out. *What the hell,* I thought. The razor would still be there when I got back. In my gut, though, it was more than that. In my gut, I felt *destined* to get out of the car.

She walked away.

I had to nearly trot to keep up. I could imagine how I must look to the people on the street: an unshaven, shambling dolt in a crushed $800 suit, hectically pursuing this . . . woman. Her high heels ticked across the cement like nails. The shiny waistcoat glittered. She took me back through the alley. Ahead, windows were lit.

"Look," she said.

Crack vials and glass crunched beneath my feet. Rotting garbage lay heaped against vomit- and urine-streaked brick.

I looked in the window, expecting to see something terrible. What I saw instead was this: A subsidized apartment,

119

sparse but clean. Two black children, a boy and a girl, sat at a table reading schoolbooks, while an aproned woman prepared dinner in the background. Then a black man walked in, a jacket over his shoulder, a lunchpail in hand. Beaming, the children glanced up. The woman smiled. The man kissed his wife, then knelt to hug his children.

But this wasn't terrible, it was wonderful. Jammed in a ghetto, surrounded by crime and despair, here was a family *making* it. Most didn't in this environment. Most fell apart against the odds. I was standing on crack vials and puke, looking straight into the face of something more powerful than any force on earth . . .

"Love," said the old woman.

Yeah, I thought. Love. I'm a lawyer, which means I'm also a nihilistic prick. You've heard the joke: What happens when a lawyer takes Viagra? He gets taller. But this made me feel good to see, the power of real love, real human ideals.

But why had the woman shown me this?

She was walking away again, and again I was huffing to keep up. Now I was curious—about her. Where did she come from? What was her name? She led me through more grimy alleys, more garbage and havens for rats. A single sodium lamp sidelighted her. My breath condensed in the cold.

I tried to look at her . . .

All I could see was one side of her face from behind. Fine lines etched her cheek and neck. Her short, straight hair was dusted with gray. Yeah, she was up there—60ish, I guessed—but elegant. You know how some women keep their looks in spite of age—that was her. Well-postured, a good figure and bosom, nice legs. But I still never really got a look at her face.

In the next alley, muttering rose.

It was getting colder. I was shivering, yet the woman seemed comfortable, she seemed warm in some arcane knowledge. She pointed down.

Aw, shit, I thought. Strewn across the alley were bundles. They were people, the inevitable detritus of any big city. They lay asleep or unconscious: shivering dark forms wrapped in newspapers or rags. Many slept convulsing from the cold. The city was too busy repaving commuter routes to build more shelters. It was astonishing that on a night this cold they didn't just freeze to death. And all this time I thought I had nothing. Jesus.

"I don't want to see this," I said.

"Wait."

I heard footsteps. Then a bent shape was moving down the dark, stepping quietly between the twitching forms. It was a priest, an old guy, 70 at least. Slung across his back were blankets. I don't know how a guy his age could manage carrying all of them, especially in cold this bad. The guy huffed and puffed, stooping to cover each prone figure with a blanket. It was the look on his face that got to me most. Not pity, not fanaticism, just some kind of resolute complacency, like he was thinking *Well, tonight I'll get whatever money I can lay my hands on, buy some blankets, and cover up some homeless people. No one else is gonna do it, so I'm gonna do it.* It was simple. Right now your average person was watching the reality shows, or getting laid, or sleeping in a warm bed, but here was this old priest doing what he could for a few people no one else gave a pinch of shit about.

"Compassion," the woman, my companion, said.

I watched as the priest went about his business, shivering himself as he lay a blanket over each figure, one after another after another. Then I touched the woman's shoulder. "What is this?" I asked. "Why are you showing me this stuff? I don't get it."

"Providence," she whispered. "Come on."

Providence, I thought. She led. I followed. Now we were

walking down Connecticut Avenue, the power drag. Lots of ritzy schmucks getting out of limos in front of restaurants where dinner for two cost more than the average working person made in two weeks. There were a lot of lawyers too, tisk, tisk. Whatever this tour was she was taking me on—it was making me think.

Next we were walking past Washington Square, where I used to work, and 21 Federal, where I stopped for cocktails every day, or had power lunches with the managing partners. Jesus. A couple of blocks away people were sleeping in the fucking street, and we were too busy to care. Too busy hiding behind Harvard law degrees and clients who paid seven figures per annum just in retainers. This bizarre woman was showing me what I used to be. And she showed me this: I may have been a good attorney, but that sure as shit didn't mean I was a good person. An hour ago I was going to kill myself. Now all I could feel was shame. I felt like a spoiled baby.

"One more stop," she said. "Then you can go."

With the less I understood, the more I wanted to know. But one thing I *did* know: There was a reason for this. This was no ordinary encounter, and she was certainly no ordinary woman.

I half trotted along, always just behind her, never quite keeping up. It reminded me of the Dickens story, the wretched cynic shown his future and past by ghosts. But the woman was no ghost. I'd touched her; she was flesh.

She was real.

Minutes later we were standing in a graveyard.

Yeah, this was like the Dickens story, all right. My breath froze in front of my face. The woman stood straight as a chess piece, pointing down at the stone. But I already knew it wasn't *my* grave.

It was my wife's.

"Truth," the woman said.

Thoughts seemed to tick in my head; my confusion felt like a fever. First love, then compassion, and now . . . truth?

What truth was there in showing me my wife's grave? She'd been dead for years.

"Does it nourish you?" the woman asked. "The truth?"

Dead for years, yeah, but even in death she was the only real truth in my life.

"I loved her," I muttered.

"Indeed. And did she love you?"

"Yes."

"Yes?"

"Yes."

She paused, gauging me, I guess. "There, then," she told me. "There's truth even in memory. You should remember her love for you—the truth of it. It raises us up, doesn't it? It *nourishes* us." Her gaze seemed to wander. "The truth."

I wanted to cry. Now this final vision made sense. I'd had love. My wife had loved me. Lots of people, most people probably, never had love, not really. Just sad facsimiles and bitter falsehoods. I wanted to fall to my knees at this old woman's feet and blubber like a little kid. Because it wasn't cruelty that made her bring me here. It was the same force behind all the things she'd shown me tonight. Things to make me think and to see. Things to make me realize that life really was a gift, and that even when people died, even when the shittiest, most fucked up things happened, the gift remained . . .

We followed back the way we came, back through the bowels of the city. It was different now—everything was. The streetlights made the pavement look gritty with ice. It began to snow but all I could feel was the warmth of what she'd shown me.

That's how I felt. I felt warm. I felt nourished.

She took me back to the alley, to the car. We got in. She sat beside me in the passenger seat.

"Time means nothing," she said. Her voice was soft, sweet in its age. "It never has."

"Who are you?" I asked.

She didn't answer. Instead she smiled, or at least she seemed to, because I still really couldn't see her. Just fragments of her, just shards of vision that never quite came together.

"You're some kind of angel, aren't you?" I finally summoned the nerve to ask. "You were sent to keep me from killing myself."

"Love, compassion, truth," she replied. "They add up to something. What a waste for a person to die alone, unnourished of the truth."

Yeah, she was an angel or something. The first thing she'd said to me was something about providence.

Greed, selfishness, cynicism, and God knows what else, had brought me to the brink of suicide but I'd been saved at the last minute by seeing the good things out there, the things that transcended the bad, the evil.

"The truth," she said.

"Thank you."

Somehow it didn't surprise me. She slipped out of the black waistcoat. She was nude beneath. Her breasts were large, with large full nipples. They sagged but gracefully. The gentle roll of flesh at her waist, the fine white skin of her throat, shoulders, and thighs, her entire body—seemed softly radiant in its age, beautiful in its truth.

That's what this was about—truth. And I knew why she'd taken off the coat. She hadn't brought me all this way just to fuck me in a Porsche 911. All night long she'd given me things to see. That's why she was naked now, to let me, at last, see *her*.

And I wanted to. I wanted to see the body which carried so resplendent a spirit. The light from the streetlamp shined through the windshield. I could see her body now, but still not her face, and I guessed I never would. This seemed appropriate, though, you've got to admit.

The face of an angel shouldn't be something you can ever really see.

"We're all here for a reason," she said, leaning over to look at me. "And this is my reason. To show the truth, to make people see the truth."

I held her hand, ran my fingers up her arm. I slid over close and began to touch her breasts, smoothed my fingers across her abdomen, down her thighs, and over the thick plot of her pubic hair. She seemed to expect this, like it was some kind of calm precognition. It wasn't lust, it wasn't sexual at all. I just wanted to touch her.

I needed to know what an angel felt like.

Her skin, though it had lost some of its elasticity, was soft and smooth as a baby's. Cool. Palely clean. The groove of her pubis sheathed my finger in heat.

Then she asked: "Are you ready to see the rest?"

"There's more?"

She paused. I think she liked this a lot, lazing back in the plush seat, being touched. "I've shown you love, compassion, and truth. I've nourished you, haven't I?"

"Yes," I said, still touching.

Her cool fingers entwined in mine. "But I need nourishment too, through something else."

"What?"

"Death," she said.

I stared at her. My hand went limp.

"The truth is like people. Sometimes the real face is the one underneath. Look now at what you didn't see before—the *rest* of the truth. The *real* truth."

She leaned over and kissed me. I turned rigid. Her cool lips played over mine, her tongue delved. All the while my eyes felt sewn open. I couldn't close them. The kiss reached into me and *pulled*. Yes, the kiss. It forced me to stare whimpering into the wide-open black chasm that was her face.

The *real* truth.

First, the future: The family in the window. The man, unemployed now, and drunk, was steadily beating his wife's face into a bleeding mask. Then, the boy, older, was holding a woman down while four others took turns raping her. He crammed a handful of garbage into her mouth to keep her quiet. "Watch me bust this bitch's coconut," he said when they were finished. He split her head open with a brick while the others divvied up her money. Meanwhile, blocks away, his sister spread her legs for the tenth stranger of the night, her arms, hands, and feet pocked by needlemarks, her blood teeming with herpes, hepatitis, AIDS.

Next, the present: The alley of the homeless. The priest was gone. A gang of faceless youths chuckled as they poured gasoline over the huddled forms, drenching the new blankets. Matches flared. The alley burst into flames, and the gang ran off, laughing. Human flesh sizzled in each cocoon of fire. Screams wheeled up into the frigid night.

And last, the past: First, brakes squealing, a collision of metal, and my wife's neck snapping like a wine stem as her head impacted the windshield. Then the vision reeled back an hour. A hotel room. A bed. Naked on hands and knees, my wife was busily fellating a young man who stood before her. He held her head and remarked, "Yeah, Duff, this is one class-A cock-suck. She's fucking me with her tonsils." "Best deep throat in town, just like I told ya," remarked another man who then promptly inserted his vaselined penis into her rectum. "Bet your hubby would shit if he could see this, huh?" Eventually he ejaculated into her bowel. "Here comes lunch," said the first man, whose semen launched into her mouth. My wife swallowed it, purring like a cat. Then she lay back on the bed. "Can you believe it? I told him I was going to the paint store to check out color schemes for the house." "When you gonna dump that limp shithead?" inquired the second man. She began masturbating them both. "Why should I?" she said. "A deal like this? Come on! He keeps me in jewelry, and you guys keep me in cock." Then the three of them burst into laughter.

The kiss broke. I seemed to fall away from it, a rappeller whose line had just been cut. I sat slack in the seat. The old woman was looking at me, but I could see she wasn't old at all. She looked like a teenager. The meal she'd made of my truth left her robust, vital, glowing in new youth. Her once-gray hair shined raven-black. The pale skin had tightened over young muscle and bone; the large white orbs of her breasts grew firm even as I watched. Their fresh nipples erected, pointing at me like wall studs.

I couldn't speak. I couldn't move.

Greedy new hands caressed me; her eyes shined. She kissed me some more, licked me, reveled in what I was to her. Her breath was hot in my drained face.

"Just a little more," she panted.

She was drooling. She reached under the seat. The Red Devil razor blade glinted in icy light. Then, very gently, she placed it in my hand.

At least it didn't hurt. It felt good. It felt purging. Know what I mean? Can't see much now. Like lights going down in a theater. All I can see is the little girl. She's watching me. She's grinning, getting younger and growing more alive on the meat of providence, on the sweet, sweet high of truth.

THE PIECE OF PAPER

When Scab hocked the bloody lump of phlegm against the wall, the actual physical effort of *heaving* caused his bladder to flinch. Some long lost instinct, then, incited him to get up and find some remote place to urinate . . . but then he remembered who he was, and his situation, and as always he just thought *Fuck it* and pissed in his pants.

See, at the same time, he remembered he had no legs.

Gone from the knees down so far, diabrotic gangrene, the doctors called it. Every six months or so, Scab rolled himself into the State Health Clinic and they'd lop off another inch.

Scab was one of Seattle's finest—a homeless sociopathic derelict. He didn't have a wheelchair—he couldn't work one due to the acute arthritis. He had a wheeled board and knuckle gloves that they gave him at the 509 annex, the halfway house on 3rd and James. Scab didn't want to live there, he just wanted the board and gloves.

The Great Outdoors was *his* terrain.

They called him Scab 'cos that's what he was covered with. Sixty-two years of disease and infections and crabs and lice and zero-hygiene and assorted dermatitis—it left its marks on a man.

Scab didn't care.

He picked the scabs off his body and ate them. They didn't taste bad, kind of like Bac-O's.

Every night was the same in a way, but Scab wasn't complaining. During the day, he'd prop himself up in front of the Borders Books on 5th, and all those freakoid hippies and commies going in to buy their *Body Piercing Review* and *High Times* and *The Revolution Sentinel* would drop endless pocket change into his cup. Scab copped about fifty bucks a day. Every now and then some tight-wad would drop in a nickel or a dime, and Scab would hock on him.

Cheapskates.

At night, he'd roll himself back between the dumpsters wedged into the alley between the Vietnamese restaurant and the King County Needle Exchange. It was a nice quiet little nook.

It was Scab's home.

And on *that* night . . .

It was raining–it always did in this butt-crack city. Scab had already rolled down the alley and parked between the dumpsters, draping himself with sheets of the *Seattle Post-Intelligencer.* Scab was drenched, sitting in his own unwashed-for-eons pants flapped over at the knees. Sitting in his own feces and urine.

Scab didn't care. It was a hard life, and if a man shit his pants, he shit his pants. At least it kept his ass warm for a while. He'd shake the shit out in the morning.

Fuck 'em, he thought. *Let 'em walk in it.*

He hoped he'd dream tonight, dream of having legs . . . and women. Rain splattered loudly on the newspaper covering his head, but just as he began to nod off, he heard . . .

Footsteps?

Scab wasn't sure. Was he dreaming?

A cute but snooty-looking woman ran down the alley. She was sopped with rain but wore a dark stuck-up businessy dress. As she ran, she hauled a briefcase.

Scab fantasized about all the great things he could do with

her, all the ways he could show her what a *real* man was when—

PAP! PAP! PAP!

Three white flashes bloomed in the alley behind the tiny noises. Scab wasn't quite sure what he was seeing but he thought—

He thought he saw the snooty-looking woman in the business dress collapse, and when the briefcase hit the pavement, it broke open. Suddenly sheets of paper began to blow around in the alley.

One such sheet landed right in Scab's lap . . .

More footsteps followed. Scab knew he was awake now, he knew this was real. Two men in suits jogged down the alley after the woman. The woman lay dead now, dark ribbons streaming away from her head in the rain.

What the fuck's goin' on? Scab wondered.

The two men in suits had slipped pistols into their jackets, and now they were frantically crawling around on their knees in the teeming rain, collecting the spilled sheets of paper. Meanwhile, a van backed into the other end of the alley. Faceless men emerged, hoisted the dead woman up, and threw her into the back.

The first two men had collected all the spilled papers. They jumped into the back of the van too, and the van squealed away.

Don't that beat fuckin' all? Scab thought.

Of course, they hadn't collected *all* of the papers–one sheet remained right there in Scab's lap. And those guys in the suits, they'd been so busy scooping up the papers, they'd never noticed Scab hidden in there between the dumpsters.

Then silence, save for the rain.

They were gone in less time than it took Scab to pick his nose.

The fuck's this? he wondered, picking up the wet piece of paper in his lap, peering at it.

The piece of paper read:

MILNET CIPHER:

READ AND DESTROY

PAGE ONE OF ONE PAGE

TELEMAIL CODE 49867-97-00/25 MAY 1978-0713 HRS
cl: TOPSECRET/SPECIALINTEL/ULTIMA/ZEBRA-000

FROM: NSA/DIRECTOR OF DOMESTIC OPERATIONS, FT. MEADE, MARYLAND
DE: LEVEL FIVE, INFECTIOUS DISEASE UNIT, FT. DEITRICK, MARYLAND
TO: IGA (INTER-AGENCY GROUP ACTIVITY) THE PENTAGON

RE: IMMUNE-SYSTEM SUPPRESSING VIRAL AGENT (LABELED CYTOMEGOLA-VIRUS "HIV") HAS NOW BEEN PERFECTED IN VITRO AT US ARMY FT. DEITRICK FACILITY.

DEPLOY STATUS: VIRUS-BASE IS READY FOR RELEASE IN LOW-INCOME URBAN LOCALES AND PERIMETERS HIGH IN IV DRUG USE AND HOMOSEXUAL ACTIVITY AS PREVIOUSLY PROSCRIBED.

PLEASE ADVISE.

END MILNET CIPHER

READ AND DESTROY

Scab stared long and hard at the piece of paper. Then he blew his nose into it, balled it up, and tossed it away.

He coughed up a few lumps of phlegm, spat them onto the side of the dumpster, then pissed his pants and fell asleep.

Of all the fuckin' things, huh?

Scab couldn't read.

THE BLURRED ROOM

(Author's Note: A modest preface seems in order here; a later version of this story was published over ten years ago as "I.C.U." in Al Sarrantonio's bestselling anth 999. Al asked me to alter my original ending (the original title had been changed by me some time before) because he felt it tipped too early and was rather cliched. These complaints are admittedly all too true, and I'll be forever grateful to Al for his editorial guidance and acceptance of the piece. But the main reason I'm including "The Blurred Room" here is for the interest of my longer-term fans, for the piece is actually one of the very first pieces of fiction (the third or fourth, perhaps) that I wrote in earnest. It's been polished a number of times, of course, but it was first composed in 1980 and later turned in to my English teacher Glen Shockley, at P.G. Community College. Mr. Shockley's encouragement regarding this piece was a salient component of my decision to become a writer.)

It chased him; it was huge. But what was it? He sensed its immensity gaining on him, pursuing him through unlit warrens, around cornerways of smothered flesh, and down alleys of ichor and blood . . .

Holy Mother of God.

When Paone fully woke, his mind felt wiped out. Dull pain and confinement crushed him, or was it paralysis? Warped images, voices, smears of light and color all massed in his head. Francis "Frankie" Paone shuddered in the terror of the nameless thing that chased him through the rabbets and fissures of his own subconscious mind.

Yes, he was awake now, but the chase led on:

Storming figures. Concussion. Blood squirting onto dirty white walls.

And like a slow-dissolve, Paone finally realized what it was that chased him. Not hitters. Not cops or feds.

It was *memory* that chased him.

But the memory of what?

The thoughts surged. *Where am I? What the hell happened to me?* This latter query, at least, shone clear. Something had happened. Something devastating . . .

The room was a blur. Paone squinted through grit teeth; without his glasses he couldn't see three feet past his face.

But he could see enough to know.

Padded leather belts girded his chest, hips, and ankles, restraining him to a bed which seemed hard as slate. He couldn't move. To his right stood a high metal pole topped by blurred blobs. A long line descended . . . to his arm. I.V. bags, he realized. The line came to an end at the inside of his right elbow. And all about him swarmed unmistakable scents: antiseptics, salves, isopropyl alcohol.

I'm in a fucking hospital, he acknowledged.

Someone must've dropped dime on him. But . . . He simply couldn't remember. The memories hovered in fragments, still chasing his spirit without mercy. Gunshots. Blood. Muzzleflash.

His myopia offered even less mercy. Beyond the bed he could detect only a vague white perimeter, shadows, and depthless bulk. A drone reached his ears, like a distant air-conditioner, and there was a slow, aggravating beep: the drip-monitor for his I.V. Overhead, something swayed. *Hanging flowerpot?* he ventured. No, it reminded him more of one of those retractable arms you'd find in a doctor's office, like an x-ray nozzle. And the fuzzed ranks of shapes along the walls could only be cabinets, pharmaceutical cabinets.

Yeah, I'm in a hospital, all right, he realized. An ICU ward. It had to be. And he was buckled down good. Not just his ankles, but his knees too, and his shoulders. More straps immobilized his right arm to the I.V. board, where white tape secured the needle sunk into the crook of his elbow.

Then Paone looked at his left arm. That's all it was—an arm. There was no hand at the end of it.

Nightmare, he wished. But the chasing memories seemed too real for a dream, and so did the pain. There was plenty of pain. It hurt to breathe, to swallow, even to blink. Pain oozed through his bowels like warm acid.

Somebody fucked me up royal, he conceded. The jail ward, no doubt. And probably a cop standing right outside the door. He knew where he was now, but it terrified him not knowing exactly what had brought him here.

The memories raged, chasing, chasing . . .

Heavy slumps. Shouts. A booming, distorted voice . . . like a megaphone.

Jesus. He wanted to remember, yet again, he didn't. The memories stalked him: pistol shots, full-auto rifle-fire, the feel of his own piece jumping in his hand.

"Hey!" he shouted. "How about some help in here!"

A click resounded to the left; a door opened and closed. Soft footsteps approached, then suddenly a bright, unfocused figure blurred toward him.

"How long have you been awake?" came a toneless, female voice.

"Couple of minutes," Paone said. Pain throbbed in his

throat. "Could you come closer? I can barely see you."

The figure obliged. Its features sharpened.

It wasn't a cop at all, it was a nurse. Tall, brunette, with fluid-blue eyes and a face of hard, eloquent lines. Her white blouse and skirt blurred like bright light. White nylons shone over sleek, coltish legs.

"Do you know where my glasses are?" Paone asked. "I'm near-sighted as hell."

"Your glasses were broken in the ambulance," she flatly replied. "The opticians are putting the lenses in new frames. They'll bring them down later."

Her vacant eyes appraised him. She leaned over to take his vitals. "How do you feel?"

"Terrible. My gut hurts like a son of a bitch, and my hand . . ." Paone, squinting, raised the bandaged left stump. "Shit," he muttered. He didn't even want to ask.

Now the nurse turned to finnick with the I.V. monitor; Paone continued to struggle against the freight of chasing memory. More images churned in some mental recess. Fragments of wood and ceiling tile raining on his shoulders. The mad cacophony of what could only be machine-gun fire. A head exploding to pulp.

Blank-faced, then, the nurse returned her gaze. "What do you remember, Mr. Paone?"

"I—" was all he said. He stared up. Paone never carried real ID on a run, and whatever he drove was either hot or chopped, with phony plates. The question ground out of his throat. "How do you know my name?"

"We know all about you," she said, unfolding a slip of paper. "The police showed me this teletype from Washington. Francis K. 'Frankie' Paone. You have seven aliases. You're 37 years old, never been married, and you have no known place of legal residence. In 1985 you were convicted of interstate flight to avoid prosecution, interstate transportation of obscene material depicting minors, and multiple violations of Section 18 of the United States Code. Two years ago you were released from Alderton Federal Peniteniary after serving 62 months of concurrent 11- and 5-year jail terms. You are a known associate of the Vinchetti crime family. You are one of the worst things in the world, Mr. Paone. You're a child pornographer."

Christ, a fuckin' burn, Paone realized. *Somebody set me up.* By now it wasn't hard to figure: lying in some ICU ward strapped to a bed, shot up like a hinged duck in a shooting gallery and one hand gone, and now this stolid bitch reading him his own rap sheet off an F.B.I fax. He sure as shit hadn't gotten busted taking down some candy store.

"You don't know what you're talking about," he said.

Her eyes were a furnace of disdain, blazing down. Her face could've been carved from stone. *Yeah,* Paone thought, *I'll bet she's got a couple kids herself flunking out of school and smoking pot. Bet her car just broke down and her insurance just went up and her hubby's late for dinner every night because he's too busy balling his secretary and snorting rails of coke off her tits, and all of a sudden it's my fault that the world's a shithouse full of perverts and pedophiles. It's my fault that a lot of people out there pay righteous cash for kiddie flicks, right, baby? Go ahead, blame me. Why not? Oh, hey, and how about the drug problem? And the recession and the Middle East and the ozone layer? That's all my fault too, right?*

Her voice sounded like she had gravel in her throat when again she asked: "What do you remember?"

The query haunted him. The bits of memory blurred along with the room in his myopic eyes (—bullets popping into flesh, the megaphone grating, spent cartridges spewing out of wafts of smoke—) and chased him further, stalking him as relentlessly as a wild cat running down a fawn, while

Paone fled on, desperate to know yet never daring to look back . . .

"Shit, nothing," he finally said. "I can't remember anything accept bits and pieces."

The nurse seemed to talk more to herself than to him. "A transient-global amnesic effect, retrograde and generally non-aphasic, induced by acute traumatic shock. Don't worry, it's a short-term symptom and quite commonplace." The big blue eyes bore back into him. "So I think I'll refresh your memory. Several hours ago, you murdered two state police officers and a federal agent."

Paone's jaw dropped.

"You're despicable," she said.

At once the chase ended, the wild cat of memory finally falling down on its prey—Paone's mind. He remembered it all, the pieces falling into place as quickly as pavement to a ledge-jumper:

The master run. Rodz. The loops.

And all the blood.

Another day, another ten K, Paone thought, mounting the three flights of stairs to Rodz' apartment. He wore jersey gloves—no way he was rockheaded enough to leave his prints anywhere near Rodz' crib. He knocked six times on the door, whistling "Love Me Tender" by The King.

"Who is it?" came the craggy voice.

"Santa Claus," Paone said. "You really should think about getting a chimney."

Rodz let him in, then quickly relocked the door. "Anyone tailing you?"

"No, just a busload of DJ agents and a camera crew from '60 Minutes.'"

Rodz glowered.

Fuck you if you can't take a joke, Paone thought. He

didn't much like Rodz—Newark slime, a whack. Nathan Rodz looked like an anorectic Tiny Tim after a bad facelift: long, frizzy black hair on the head of a pudgy medical cadaver, speedlines down his cheeks. Rodz was what parlance dubbed a "snatch-cam"—a subcontractor, so to speak. He abducted the kids, or got them on loan from freelance movers, then shot the tapes himself. "The Circuit" was what the justice department called the business: underground pornography. It was a 1.5-billion-dollar-per-year industry that almost no one knew about, a far cry from the "Debbie Does Dallas" bunk you rented down at the XXX store. Paone muled all kinds of underground: rape loops, "wet" S&M, animal flicks, scat, snuff, and (their biggest number) "kp" and "prepubes." Paone picked up the masters from guys like Rodz, then muled them to Vinchetti's mobile "dupe" lab. Vinchetti's network controlled almost all of the underground porn in the east; Paone was the middleman, part of the family. It all worked through mail-drops and coded distro points. Vinchetti paid two grand for a 20-minute master if the resolution was good; from there each master was dupped hundreds of times and sold to clients with a taste for the perverse. "Logboys," the guys who did the actual rodwork, were hired freelance on the side; that way, nobody could spin on Vinchetti himself. Paone had seen some shit in his time—part of his job was to sample each master for quality: biker chicks on PCP blowing horses and dogs, addicts excreting on each other and often consuming the produce of their bowels. "Nek" flicks, "Bag" flicks. Logboys getting down on pregnant girls, retarded girls, amputees and deformees. And snuff. It amazed Paone, in spite of its outright horror: people *paid* to see this stuff. They got off on it. *What a fucked up world,* he thought a million times over, but, hey, supply and demand—that was the American Way, wasn't it? If Vinchetti didn't supply the clients, someone else would, and as long as the money was there . . .

I'll take my cut, Paone stonily thought.

The biggest orders were always for kp. According to federal stats, 10,000 kids disappeared each year and were never seen again; most of them wound up in The Circuit. The younger the kids, the more the tapes cost. Once a kid got old (14 or 15) they were deemed as "beat," and they were either sold overseas, or put out on the street to turn tricks for Vinchetti's pross net. One thing feeding the other. Yeah, it was a fucked up world, all right, but that wasn't Paone's problem. His job was simple: he bought the masters, muled them to the lab and kept the snatch-cams in line—guys like this muck-for-brains short-eyed scumbag Rodz.

"I got five for ya," said Rodz, "the usual." Rodz' voice was more annoying than nails across slate, a nasally, wet rasp. "But I been thinking, you know?"

"Oh, you think?" Paone asked. He'd never seen such a pit for an apartment. Little living room full of put-it-together-yourself furniture, smudged walls, tacky green and brown carpet tile; an odiferous kitchen. *Buckingham Fucking Palace this ain't.*

"Like two K a pop is getting pretty skimpy these days," Rodz went on. "Come on, man, for a fucking master that Vinchetti's crew'll dupe hundreds of times? That's serious green for him. But what about me? Everytime I make a master for your man, I'm sticking my neck out a mile."

"That's because you were born with a mile-long neck, Ichabod."

"I think two-point five at least is fair. I mean, I heard that the Bonte family's paying three."

Paone stared him down. "Watch that, Rodz. No jive. You master for Vinchetti and Vinchetti only. Period. You want some advice? Don't even think about peddling your shit to some other family. The last guy who pulled a stunt like that, you know what happened to him? Jersey cops found him hanging upside-down in some apartment laundry room. Blowtorched. And they cut off his cock and Express Mailed it to his grandmother in San Bernardino."

Rodz' face did a twitch. "Yeah, well, like I was saying, two K a pop sounds pretty square."

I thought so, Paone regarded.

"So where's that green?"

Paone headed toward the back bedroom, where Rodz did his thing. "You don't touch doggie-doo till I see the fruits of your labor."

He sat down on a couch that had no doubt served as a prop in dozens of Rodz' viddies. High-end cameras and lights sat on tripods, not the kind of gear they sold down at Radio Shack. The masters had to be shot on large-format inch-and-a-quarter high-speed tape so the dupes retained good contrast. The five boxed tapes sat before a 35" Sony Trinitron and a studio double-player by Thompson Electronics. "Good kids this time, too," Rodz complimented himself. "All level." Sometimes a kid would freak on camera, or space out; lots of them were screwed-up from the get-go: Fetal Cocaine babies, Fetal Alcohol Syndrome, Battered Child Syndrome. There were times when Paone actually felt sad about the way things worked.

Now came the sadder part: Paone had to sit back and watch each master; lighting, resolution, and clarity all had to be good. He plugged in the first tape . . .

Jesus, he thought. Pale movement flickered on the screen. They were always the same in a way. What bothered Paone most were the faces—the forlorn, tiny faces on the kids, the look while Rodz' stunt cocks got busy. *What do they think?* Paone wondered. *What goes on in their heads?* Every so often the kid would look into the camera and offer a stare that defied description . . .

"At least let me UV the cash while you're watching," Rodz said.

"Yeah, yeah." Paone threw him the stuffed envelope. His face felt molded of clay as he watched on. Rodz always fronted his flicks with cutesy titles, like "Vaseline Alley," "The Young And The Hairless," "Stomper Room." Meanwhile Rodz himself donned nylon gloves and took out the band of century notes. Ten grand didn't look like much. He scanned each bill front and back with a Sirchie ultraviolet lamp. Technicians from Treasury worked liaison with DJ and the Bureau all the time. Their favorite game was to turn someone out and dust buy-money with invisible uranyl phosphate dyes. Dead solid perfect in court.

"Clean enough for ya?" Paone asked, "I mean, a clean guy like yourself?"

"Yeah, looks good." Rodz face looked lit up as he inspected the bills. "Unsequenced numbers too. That's great."

Paone winced when he glanced back to the screen. In the last tape, here was Rodz' himself, with his hair pulled back and a phony beard, doing the rodwork himself. Paone frowned.

"Sweet, huh?" Rodz grinned at himself on the screen. "Always wanted to be in pictures."

"You should get an Oscar. Best Supporting Pervert."

"It's some fringe bennie. And look who's talking about pervert. I just make the tapes. It's your people who distribute them."

Rodz had a point. *I'm just a player in the big game,* Paone reminded himself. *When the money's good you do what you gotta do.*

"I'm outa here," Paone said when the last master flicked off. He packed up the tapes and followed Rodz out to the living room. "I wish I could say it's been a pleasure."

Rodz chuckled. "You should be nicer to me. One day I might let you be in one of my flicks. You'd never be the same."

"Yeah? And you'll never be the same when I twist your head off and shove it up your ass."

By the apartment door, Rodz held the speedlined grin. "See you next time . . . I'd offer to shake hands except I wouldn't want to get any slime on you."

"Thanks for the thought." Paone polished his glasses with a handkerchief, reached for the door, and—

Ka-CRACK!

"Holy shit!" Rodz yelled.

—the door blew out of its frame. Not kicked open, knocked down, and it was no wonder when Paone, in a moment of static shock, noted the size of the TSD cop stepping back with the steelhead door-ram. An even bigger cop three-pointed into the room with a cocked revolver.

"Freeze! Police!"

Paone moved faster than he'd ever moved in his life, got an arm around Rodz, and began to jerk back. Rodz gasped, pissing his pants, as Paone used him as a human shield. Two shots rang out, both of which socked into Rodz' upper sternum.

"Give it up, Paone!" the cop advised. "There's no way out!"

Bullshit, Paone thought. Rodz twitched, gargling blood down his front, then suddenly turned to dead weight. But the move gave Paone time to duck behind the kitchen counter and shuck his SIG 220 chock full of 9mm hardball. *Move fast!* he directed himself, then sprang up, squeezed off two rounds, and popped back down. Both slugs slammed into the cop's throat. All Paone heard was the slump.

Shadows stiffened in the doorway. A megaphone boomed: "Francis Frankie Paone, you're surrounded by justice department agents and the state police. Throw down your weapon and surrender. Throw down your weapon and surrender, throw down your—" and on and on.

Paone shucked his back-up piece—an ice-cold Colt snub—and tossed it over the counter. Another state cop and a guy in a suit blundered in. *Dumb fucks,* Paone thought. He sprang up again, squeezed off two sets of doubletaps. The cop twirled, taking both bullets in the chin. And the suit, a DJ agent, took his pair between the eyes. In the frantic glimpse, Paone had time to see the guy's head explode. A goulash of brains slapped the wall.

No way I'm going down. Paone felt surprisingly calm. *Back room. Window.* Three-story drop into the bushes. It was his only chance . . .

But a chance he'd never get.

Before he could move out, the room began to . . . vibrate.

Three state SWAT men in kevlar charged almost balletically into the room, and after that the world turned to chaos. Bullets swept toward Paone in waves. M-16's on full-auto spewed hot brass and rattled away like lawnmowers, rip-stitching holes along the walls, tearing the kitchen apart. "I give up!" Paone shouted but the volley of gunfire only increased. He curled up into a ball as everything around him began to disintegrate into flying bits. Clip after clip, the bullets came, bursting cabinets, chewing up the counter and the floor, and when there was little left of the kitchen, there wasn't much left of Paone. His left hand hung by a single sinew. Hot slivers of steel cooked in his guts.

Then: silence.

His stomach burned like swallowed napalm. His consciousness began to drift away with wafts of cordite. He sidled over; blood dotted his glasses. EMT's carried off the dead police as a man in blue utilities poked forward with a smoking rifle barrel. Radio squawk eddied foglike in the hot air, and next Paone was being stretchered out over what seemed a lake of blood.

Dreamy moments later, red and white lights beat in his eyes. The doors of the ambulance slammed shut.

"Great God Almighty," he whispered.

"I'd told you you'd remember," the nurse said.

"How bad am I shot?"

"Not bad enough to kill you. I.V. antibiotics held off the peritoneal infection." Her eyes narrowed. "Lucky for you there's no death penalty in this state."

That's right, Paone slowly thought. And the fed statutes only allowed capital punishment if an agent was killed during a narcotics offense. They'd send him up for life with no parole, sure, but that beat fertilizing the cemetery. The fed slams were easier than a lot of the state cuts; plus, Paone was a cop-killer, and cop-killers got instant status in stir. No bulls would be trying to bust his cherry. *Things could be worse,* he recognized now. He remembered what he'd told that punk Rodz about taking things for granted; Paone stuck to his guns. He was busted, shot up like swiss cheese, and had left one of his hands on Rodz' kitchen floor, but at least he was alive. And who knew? If he used his smarts and took his time, he might even be able to bust out of stir someday.

Yeah, he thought. *Hope springs eternal.*

"What are you smiling about?" the nurse asked.

"I don't know. Just happy to be alive, I guess . . . Yeah, that's it." It was true. Despite these rather irrefutable circumstances, Paone was indeed very happy.

"Happy to be alive?" The nurse looked coldly disgusted. "What about the men you murdered? They had wives, families. They had children. Those children are fatherless now. Those men are dead because of you."

Paone shrugged as best he could. "Life's a gamble. They lost and I won. They're the ones who wanted to play hardball, not me. If they hadn't fucked with me, their kids would still have daddies. I'm not gonna feel guilty for wasting a bunch of guys who tried to take me down."

"You make me sick," the nurse said.

I love you too, baby. It was ironic. The pain in his gut sharpened yet Paone couldn't help his exuberance. He wished he had his glasses so he could see the nurse better. Hell, he wished he had a cold beer too, and a smoke. He wished he wasn't in these damn hospital restraints. A little celebration of life seemed in order, like maybe he wouldn't mind putting the blocks on this ice-bitch nurse. *Yeah, like maybe bend her big can over these bed rails and give that cold pussy of hers a good working over. Bet that'd take some of the starch out of her sails.*

Paone, next, began to actually laugh. What a weird turn of the cards the world was. God worked in strange ways, all right. *At least He's got a sense of humor.* It was funny. *Those three cops bite the dust and I'm lying here all snug and cozy, gandering the Ice Bitch.* Paone's low and choppy laughter did not abate.

The nurse turned on the radio to drown out her patient's unseemly jubilation. Light news filled the air as she checked Paone's pulse and marked his I.V. bags. The newscaster droned the day's paramount events: The Japanese were going to start importing U.S. cars. Zero-fat butter to hit the market next week. The Surgeon General was imploring manufacturers to suspend production of silicon testicular implants, and the president (—Oh, goodness no!—) had the flu. It made things even funnier: the world and all its silliness suddenly meant nothing to Paone. He was going to the slam. What difference did anything, good or bad, make to him now?

He squinted up when another figure came in. Through the room's blurred features, a face leaned over: a sixtyish guy, snow-white hair and a great bushy mustache. "Good evening, Mr. Paone," came the greeting. "My name's Dr.

Willet. I wanted to stop by and see how you're doing. Is there anything I can get for you?"

"Since you asked, doc, I wouldn't mind having my glasses back, and to tell you the truth I wouldn't mind having another nurse. This one here's about as friendly as a mad dog."

Willet only smiled in response. "You were shot up pretty bad but you needn't worry now about infection or blood loss. Those are always our chief concerns with multiple gunshot wounds. I'm happy to inform you that you're in surprisingly good shape considering what happened."

Jolly good, Paone thought.

"And I must say," Willet went on, "I've been anxious to meet you. You're the first murderer I've ever had the opportunity to speak with. In a bizarre sense, you're famous. The renegade outlaw."

"Well, I'd offer to give you an autograph," Paone joked, "but there's a problem. I'm left-handed."

"Good, good, that's the spirit. It's a man of character who can maintain a sense of levity after going thought what you've—"

"Shhh!" the nurse hissed. She seemed jittery now, a pent-up blur. "This is it . . . I think this is it."

Paone made a face. From the radio, the newscaster droned on: ". . . in a year-long federal sting operation. One suspect, Nathan Rodz, was killed on site in a frantic shootout with police. Two state police officers and one special agent from the department of justice were also killed, according to authorities, by the second suspect, an alleged mob middleman by the name of Francis 'Frankie' Paone. Paone himself was under investigation for similar allegations, and thought to have direct ties with the Vinchetti crime family, which is said to control over fifty-percent of all child pornography marketed in the U.S. Police spokesmen later announced that Paone received massive gunshot wounds to the abdomen and was reported dead on arrival at South Arundel County Medical Center . . ."

Paone's thoughts seemed to slowly flatten. "What's this . . . Dead on arrival?"

The nurse was smiling now. She opened a pair of black-framed glasses and put them on Paone's face . . .

The blurred room, at last, came into focus.

Aw, Jesus God—

It wasn't an x-ray nozzle that hung overhead; it was a pan scale. Shiny white tiles covered the walls. Paone now clearly recognized that the "pharmacuetical" cabinets were actually flanks of metal shelves stacked merely with buckets and bottles. One bucket was labeled HISTOLOGY. Another label read: FORMALIN. And still another: PITUITARIES. Last but not least, the floor (—mere bare gray cement—) had a drain in the middle of it.

—sweet Jesus and God in heaven, Paone's thoughts finished.

This wasn't a hospital. This wasn't an intensive-care unit.

This is the morgue, Paone realized.

And as the nurse taped shut Paone's mouth, Dr. Willet selected a particularly long bivalving knife from a tray of assorted instruments. It flashed in the light when he held it up.

"Time for your autopsy, Mr. Paone," the pathologist announced. His face seemed pleasant; his eyes beamed. "And I can promise that I'll do my very best to see that you remain alive for as long as possible."

Paone shuddered as Willet commenced with the first incision.

GUT-SHOT

Eliot and Snydicker were talking about it once. It's why smart cops never eat before a shift. Less semi-digested material in the intestinal tract. The skell were loading teflon bullets now, since that article in the *Post*. Nine-mil would punch right through Threat-Level 2 Kevlar. Peritonitis is slow death, especially back in 1981 before the new class of anti-biotics. Fecal bacteria directly invades the bloodstream, overwhelming all immune-system response. Absolute abdominal infection.

The party:
"Cop over in Capitol Heights got gut-shot the other night," one of the Road Hogs says. Now, you don't even remember her name, so you'll call her Nameless. Road Hogs is parlance for Cop Groupies; the girls always seem to work at 7-Elevens near police stations. You never understand the attraction, since most cops—yourself included—are head cases.

"Yeah," Jackson concurs, slurping his tenth National Bo. "I know the guy, guy named Foster. Bunch'a PCP cowboys gut-shot him right in front of the Safeway they were trying to rob. P.G. County TAC squad took 'em all out a couple hours later. Tried to take hostages at fuckin' Arby's."

You gulp. "What happened to Foster?"

"He's in intensive care. They're giving him fifty-fifty." Jackson leans drunkenly forward, the preceptor guiding the student. "That's what he gets for not wearing his vest, Seymour. Always wear your vest."

You never wear your vest, not in the summer, because no one else does. It's too hot and it makes your skin break out. Besides, you don't want the rest of the force to think you're a pussy.

"But you never wear yours," you point out.

"Don't do as I do, Seymour. Do as I say."

"He's drunk," Nameless whispers in your ear. Her hand creeps up your leg, and her bosom is pressing you. An 8mm porn movie flickers on a smudged pull-down screen in the corner but no one pays much attention; there's just the soft flittering sound. *Gut-shot*, you think. Everyone else—the girls and the other cops—are in the back rooms.

"My first year on the force," Jackson goes on, "I popped four Super-Vels into a crank-head. You know what the motherfucker does?"

"Oh, Jaxie, give it a rest!" Nameless insists. Now she's practically cupped your crotch right there on the beer-stained couch. The porn movie flitters and flitters, a grainy blonde with crystal-meth eyes jacking sperm out of a penis stout as your L-25 nightstick.

"The motherfucker gets up and pops me back with a Ruger .22, put four right in the breadbasket." Jackson indecorously lifts his t-shirt, showing the scars. "Gut-shot me. I almost died. For two weeks it felt like I had a belly full of red-hot rivets. Was on disability for a fuckin' year and a half."

You gulp again, the rookie in dread.

Jackson crumples his empty beer can and scowls at you. "What do you wanna be a cop for, Seymour? You out'a your mind?"

It was a good question.

Jackson would eventually be kicked off the force and sentenced to a year in P.G. County detent for child molestation.

And you never got your chance with Nameless that night. Some drunk transit cop walked in and took her into the back.

Three weeks later:

Is it an augur's whisper in the dead or night, or just simple fear? You know you're going to get killed if you ignore the premonition. You know you'll be gut-shot.

You got the call five minutes before shift-change, got your first chance to see the P.G. County Morgue.

"How do you like that?" Chief Williamson says with some mirth. "The rookie finally gets his very own Signal 64! The decedent was murdered behind at the tile factory on Bladensburg Road. That's our juris, Seymour. And guess what that means?"

"I don't know," you answer but you're already feeling the ineffable chill.

"That means *you* get to examine the body for signs of violence."

Williamson, with a wide pumpkin grin, opens the metal door. Red stenciled letters read AUTHORIZED PERSONEL ONLY and you immediately notice that they've misspelled personnel. The door creaks and fetid cold air slips out; it's almost a cliché. The Chief is loving this. His expression seems to say: Come in to my parlor . . .

It's not like on TV. You expect a wall of sliding drawers but there're only tables. On one table there's a small Parke-Davis body bag less than a yard long. *The baby murdered in Seat Pleasant last night,* it occurs to you. *Drowned in a laundry tub.* Another table contains a pile of black plastic bags: pieces.

"Grab me a Coke out of the fridge, will ya?" the Chief requests.

Half-dizzy, you open the refrigerator only to recoil. On the middle shelf lay a plastic zip-lock bag containing one severed human foot.

"Got'cha!" the Chief bellows and busts out laughing.

Your stomach clenches. You're not laughing. "Come on, son, we ain't got all night," Williamson prods you. Now you re-face the center of the room, the tables. Many are empty but two in the back are draped over. "Which one's ours, Chief?"

"Not *ours*," he reminds. "*Yours*. But let's see . . ." Two white bony feet protrude from one of the covers. "Could it be this one?" and then the Chief dramatically whips back the sheet. Lying beneath is a dead young woman, mid-'20s probably but she looks fifty. She's nude, y-sectioned, spread out on the table like a raw stromboli.

"Oh no!" the Chief mocks. "It's Seymour's prom date!"

"Funny, boss."

"Go for a quickie? I won't tell. And at least you won't have to call her tomorrow!"

"Yeah, *real* funny." You try to avert your eyes but can't. Fish-belly-white skin stretched over bones. Her head looks like a skull with a dirty blond wig on it. Lividity has turned her nipples and lips the color of plums. "So is she the one or isn't she?"

The Chief ignores the query. "And would you look at the snatch on her? Looks like someone dropped an ax in the middle of a woodchuck." Williamson's voice softens. "Can you imagine it, Seymour? Can you imagine stickin' your johnson into a big mess like that?"

You exhale deep, close your eyes. "Is she the one or not?"

"Naw." The Chief re-covers her with the sheet. "Just wanted to give you your first gander of junkie corpse. You'll see a lot of 'em. This one OD'd over at Colmar Manor. Word is the EMTs drove extra slow so she'd croak before they got her back to the ER. Good for them, I say. Saves our tax dollars." He approaches the next table. "Naw, Seymour, it's this one here. Here's your 64." He whips back the sheet to expose a long gaunt black man, also naked. His skin looks like caramel wax in the overhead fluorescents, a macabre museum dummy.

A massive shotgun wound has ground up the cadaver's abdomen.

"Here's your man, rookie. You take it from here."

You wince. "I'm supposed to . . . *what?*"

"Make a close visual inspection of the corpse. Check for signs of violence."

"Signs of violence?" you close to yell. "He's gut-shot! It seems to me that the obvious twelve-gauge blast to the belly is all the 'signs of violence' we need!"

"Negatory, Seymour." The Chief hands you a pair of examination gloves and a magnifying glass. "Gotta check everything. Every square inch of the body for accessory evidence. Knife wounds, needle marks, contusions—shit like that. And when I say everywhere, Seymour, I mean everywhere. The cock, the balls. Nostrils, inside the mouth, inside the ears, the ass-crack."

First you gape at the gloves and magnifier, then you gape back at the Chief. "Jesus Christ, Chief! I don't want to check this guy's *ass-crack!* You're shitting me, right?"

"No jive. Every square inch. If he's got needle marks on him, for instance, then that tells us that the crime was drug-related."

Revolted, you snatch up the case board. "That would be in the tox screen, Chief. The ME's already prelim'd this guy and waived autopsy. Cause of death is established. And now I gotta check his *ass-crack* with a fucking *magnifying glass?*"

"'Fraid so, son. We need that info for our own report to the county."

"Aw, Jesus . . ."

"Hey," the Chief chuckles. "You're the one who wanted to be a cop."

You snap on the gloves, bewildered. You begin to lean over the cadaver. The odor of excrement wafts up from the catastrophic wound.

"Check the dick first, and around under the balls. Look for herpes and shit like that."

The stench is extraordinary. You eye the magnifier and simultaneously reach out to touch the penis and scrotum of a dead man.

"Got'cha!" the Chief bellows and busts out laughing. "I'm just pullin' your legs, kid. Ho boy, you should've seen the look on your face as you were reaching for the cock!"

You're too relieved to get pissed. "Funny, Chief. Real funny." You snap off the gloves and drop them in a pedal-operated garbage can full of plastic bags marked DISPOSABLE MATERIAL.

"Just wanted to give you your first look at the morgue, Seymour, so you'll know what to expect next time. Technical familiarization, you know? Oh, and I've already booked you for an autopsy. Next week. It's something you'll need to see."

"Thanks," you grumble.

"Come on, let's go get some coffee and Suzy-Q's!"

Suzy-Q's, you think. *Terrific.* But as you shuffle out behind him, he adds, "So what did tonight teach you, Seymour?"

Something unbidden forces you to stop. Turn back around. Look again at the draped corpse. "Uhhhhhhhh," you stall.

"Always wear your vest," the Chief answers for you. "Otherwise you'll get gut-shot and wind up like that guy on the slab."

The Chief, naturally, isn't wearing his own vest. He never does.

"Then how come you're not wearing yours?" you say.

Williamson echoes Jackson's words. "Don't do as I do. Do as I say."

Midnight. Off-shift.

It's been a tough day but an interesting one. You stop D.C. rush hour simply by holding up your hand. You arrest a guy who's got multiple bench warrants out on him. You help an old man who's locked his keys in his car, and you slap a cigarette out of a punk's mouth and make him dump his beer into the gutter. Then there was the ghoulish trip to the morgue.

You always wanted to be a cop, so here you are. Free coffee, road hogs, and a six-inch Colt Trooper Mark III on your hip. Yeah, you got to slap a cigarette out of a punk's mouth today, but you're really just a punk yourself.

Nameless has her top off and your pants down. She's proving a formidable expertise. Her breasts overflow in your hands. So this is what it's all about, huh? Fellatio from groupies and the power of arrest. Almost all the lights are out in the seedy apartment; an occasional draft of warm summer-night air slips in through a window propped open by a copy D.M. Thomas' *The White Hotel.* You think you might want to write books yourself one day . . . but how can you really do that? You're a police officer, not a writer.

As the mouth moves down harder and hotter, you wonder what you might be missing if you never write: the honor of having your *own* books being used to prop open windows.

A wet click, then: "Come on, get it . . ."

You've wanted Nameless since the first moment you saw her. She was bent over fixing the Slurpee machine, her big plush butt jutting. "Best head queen this side of the district line," Diginzio from Seat Pleasant remarked when you walked in. "Why bother jerking off when you can just stick it her mouth and leave the mess. She's Human Kleenex." You think it's funny at the time but the fact is she's had a miserable life, and you and all these other asshole town-clown cops just want to make it *more* miserable.

But you're ready to go, just then, in the dark, on the half-busted couch with springs sticking out. You're ready to put it all into the Human Kleenex. Your indoctrination—something to yuk-up about tomorrow at the station house. Yeah, this is what it's all about, all right . . . .

You don't believe in premonitions, nor in ghosts. You're half-drunk so you have to concentrate, squeeze your eyes shut and think about the last stripper you saw at Star-Light because, well, Nameless isn't really much to look at.

"Come on . . . ."

But you imagine it's not her voice. You open your eyes and see—or think you see—a figure standing in the coat closet. A gaunt naked black man with a belly torn up by 12-gauge. Suddenly you can smell the morgue-cool shit eddying from his gut.

Your cock not only goes instantly limp, it seems to retract into your groin.

Nameless is up, an abrupt shadow. She's pulling her blouse on. She's sobbing.

"I know, I know! I'm fat and ugly! Jesus Christ!"

You sit stupefied, heart thudding. "No, it's not you, I just drank too much is all, I—"

"I'm a *pig!*" she sobs.

"No, you're not a—"

"I know! I know what you fucking guys say about me! And it's true!"

"No, really—"

She rushes to her bedroom, slams and locks the door. You can still hear her crying.

Come on . . .

You pull up your pants, grab your gun belt, and leave as fast as you can. But not before shining your Kel-Lite into the closet where there's nothing but a few coats.

Driving home on Bladensburg Road in your slate-green Pinto, listening to King Crimson on a fucking 8-track. A cop driving drunk. The moon follows you, glimpses you between drab buildings like a jeering face. You know you don't believe in premonitions, and you know you don't believe in ghosts (you won't believe in any of that for two more decades) but when you pass the old labyrinthine tile factory, isn't there one single window lit against the entire brick mass? Isn't it a gaunt naked black man looking out? No, probably just a security guard or custodian.

You quit at the end of the summer. You'd rather be a writer and, besides, a police department is no place for a shit-scared kid. The man who replaces you is a former EPS officer named Hulligan, and he gets gut-shot checking out the tile factory during his first week on the job.

MAKE A WISH

"Look," Jessy said. "A falling star."

Why did her gaze upward seem so hopeful? In Seattle, the stars always looked further away than they had in Baltimore; Spad said it was because they were closer to the North Pole. At first, she could barely make it out: a tiny fleck of light that streaked across the midnight sky over Elliot Bay. "Can you see it?" she asked.

Spad managed a smile. "Make a wish. But you have to make it quick, before the star burns out."

But Jessy didn't believe in wishes. Why should she?

The twenty-dollar bags of "boy" were long gone. Skag was cheaper here—lumps of sticky black tar from Mexico. They sold it in "quarters" for quarter grams, and it was only ten bucks a bang. It was also much more potent. Even with the resistence she'd built up, in Seattle she could get both get by on six a day, even four. Everything she'd heard in the Baltimore County lock-up had turned out to be true . . . at least with regard to heroin. On the west coast, it was better, stronger, cheaper, and easier to cop. The needle exchanges were legit: no questions asked. Supply never turned dry. But then there were the things they *hadn't* mentioned. You abscessed with each and every shot. The stuff stayed black when you strained it; it was like

158

injecting dirt into yourself, and you had to muscle half your hits because your blood coagulated faster. Your whole body scabbed up after a while, and it was ten times harder to turn tricks in this town. Jessy'd always figured you had to take the good with the bad anywhere in life, but here the bad snuck up on you and then put you down like a brick that fell off the top floor of the SeaFirst Building and landed on your head. Every day when she woke up to cop, she wished she was dead. Being dead seemed so much easier. Out here junkies and crackheads jumped off the Aurora bridge two a week. No one had survived yet.

But she couldn't do that now. She was pregnant.

"Jessy's got herself a little smack-baby comin'," Leon had told her the other day when he'd gotten out of jail. She was starting to show, her 95-pound frame sporting a tight shiny pot-belly. "If this one lives," Leon had said, "give it to me. I know people who buy babies. They won't know it's all fucked up till later. It ain't really a kid, Jess. It's a junk-baby, it's like takin' a shit. Come on, I'll give ya twenty bucks for it." *Fuck you,* she thought. Leon had been her pimp when she'd first arrived three years ago. He'd been smiling down at her when she'd stepped off the 194 bus; he knew. But he'd kicked her out of the crib after only a few months, and knocked several teeth out as a going-away present. "You're a waste'a my time, bitch. That shit's uglied you up so bad, you scare all rummies out'a Piss Park." But she'd been pregnant before—three times—and she'd always miscarriaged. It was either the skag or malnutrition, or both.

She'd worked her way down fast. Never "pretty" to begin with, her face was slightly elongated and eyes too far apart—the Fetal Alcohol Syndrome was all that she'd ever inherit from her mother—and now the black skag just made it worse. The scabs flecked her face like a leprosy. Makeup wouldn't cover them, and if she picked them off, they'd just bleed for hours and re-form larger. On some occasions, though, she'd get lucky, when johns picked her up on Jackson Street too drunk to notice what she looked like, but mostly she'd been relegated to the bum bars, the bottom of the trick barrel. They didn't care. The down-side was they always spent their SSI money within a week of the first of the month, then it was gone. Grueling blow-jobs behind bus stops, between dumpsters, in urine-drenched alleys. At least in Baltimore she'd had steady tricks.

Each day progressed like slow drool. Perpetually constipated, dizzy from low blood sugar, half-paralyzed from initial withdrawal. She felt weightless, a husk in dirty jeans and flip-flops. Her zombie-like trek led her through downtown's bowels while she pleaded to a god she didn't believe in for just one scumbag to blow for twenty dollars. Unless you could prove state residency, the rehabs would back-burner you. Three to six months. How can we reach you when a slot opens? Oh, just give me a call; I live under the trolley bridge at 4th and Jackson. Bridge-surfing was easier; to get a bed at a shelter you either had to camp out (in which case the cops rousted you) or bribe a counselor. Instead of leaving the King Dome up to at least keep the homeless out of the rain, they'd demolitioned it for a new stadium they couldn't possibly pay for, and the latest "beautify downtown" plan closed two more shelters.

Fuck it. She'd wash in Lake Union and sleep under bridges.

Dumpster-diving kept her fed and pan-handling could generally cover a couple of bangs a day—then it was on to the bars and the alleys. Surprisingly, none of her four pregnancies had been from johns. Even before the eruption of black-tar scabs, ninety-nine percent of her tricks were just quick blow-jobs in cars. Instead, her pregnancies had resulted from a multitude of rapes. At night, the animals assumed their turf. Between the psychotic bums in Piss Park and the gangs north of 9ᵗʰ street, Jessy was mere sexual meat whenever her addiction forced her across these lines. She'd nearly been killed once by several members of some gang called the Kay-Mob. "Never seed me a ho THAT ugly!" she'd heard. They were about to crack her head open with a two-by-four after an hour-long train behind the Aristocrat. "Bust the bitch's coconut!" But they'd fled when a car pulled into the lot. Jessy had seen in the headlights that none of them could've been older than fifteen.

She could never understand it. Even in all her hardship, and in all the appalling things she'd witnessed, she could never understand how people could be so monstrous, so absolutely evil.

Each miscarriage felt like a disembowelment, and they'd come with the quickness of rifle shots. There was nothing she could do but leave them there and run away shrieking into rainy darkness. Killing herself seemed mouth-watering, like a box of bon-bons being viewed by a fat boy through the candy-store window. But the skag would never let her. It was always "I'll just cop one more time, then do it," but she knew that that one more time would last forever.

Not caring was her only source of vengeance. The Red Chinese spies stealing military secrets? Forty-car collision on I-5 kills twelve? Wild fires in the mid-west scorch 100,000 acres and leave hundreds homeless? So what? The world didn't care about her. Why should she care about the world?

Spad seemed to care, though.

She'd met him a year ago. She'd tried to steal a flower from the market—one of those phony red-satin roses. The security guards had chased her all the way down the Pike's Market Hillclimb and across the train tracks before they'd given up. A few minutes later, though, Spad appeared in a dingy pea-coat with a TeleTubbie on the sleeve. "After all that, you definitely deserve these," he said, and gave her a handful of the phony roses.

He was just like her in a way: looking for something when there was nothing left to look for—only he hadn't given up. He was slim and handsome, and didn't abscess nearly as badly as most. He taught her to always use the surplus insulin syringes from the exchange; they hurt more but you could always sense the vein more precisely. Spad was smart. He was interested in things, and this fascinated her. Everyday he'd jimmy open a paper box and read the *Times*, but he'd always put it back when he was done. He even believed in God. "We're all spirits, Jessy," he told her once. "We're immortal. When we die, God saves us."

"Well why doesn't He fucking save us now?" she argued back. "How could God put us in a shitty world like this?"

"God didn't make the world shitty, we did. But don't worry. He'll forgive us."

For some reason, this sounded hopeful to her, or perhaps she was just impressed by his ability to hope at all.

Spad got a lot more tricks than she did, but he always shared the money with her. Once he'd ripped off a john just so he could rent them a room for one night at the Bush; it was her birthday. The lumpy bed felt like heaven. He taught her how to have fun. During the WTO riots, they gleefully tore through the crowds and picked protestors' pockets. They'd moon police from the Jackson overpass and steal pizzas from the Pagliacci's on Stone Way because they always left the back door open. They'd hang on to the back rails of the waterfront street car and laugh in the breeze. Even in their mutual curse, Spad taught her to laugh.

Then he began to die.

Of course, in a sense, they both were, and they knew it, but Spad's AIDS made the notion much more immediate. The sarcoma on his back and the backs of his legs told them all they needed to know. "It's not that big a deal," he'd said earlier on, smiling. "My only worry is how are you going to steal pizzas without me?" Jessy's grief bottled her up; she didn't know how to deal with all those black emotions at once. She'd never cry in front of him–that would make him feel dead already. Soon it was up to her to cop for both of them, and she didn't do very well. At least in the summer she could make more pan-handling, from the tourists, but it was nearly impossible to leave him. Her worst fear was that she'd come back to the bridge with a couple quarter grams and he'd be dead. She'd be alone. What would she do then? She supposed she could kill herself by his side, but what of the baby? No, she couldn't do that. Nothing was fair, ever.

Meanwhile, he got sicker and sicker, to the point that he could barely move most of the time. On a good day, though–like today–he managed to walk with her down to the waterfront. She pan-handled all day in front of the Red Robin's while he slept beneath the abutments of the public pier. She made over forty dollars, then she went back to him . . .

"Did you make your wish?" he asked. He looked like a skeleton in rotten clothes, and he'd been coughing up more blood. Somehow, though, he seemed at ease.

"No such thing as wishes."

"Of course there is. You made forty dollars today."

"I didn't wish for it. It just happened."

"Are you sure about that?"

"Yes!" Her voice sounded like a stranger's, bitchy, argumentative. She couldn't bring herself to look at him. So she looked up at the sky.

The falling star was still there, a streaking white fleck over the mountains beyond the Sound. There was a naval post over there, in Bremerton, and she'd always heard it was a good place to turns tricks. Other girls would tell her that if you hitchhiked the main drag after midnight, the servicemen would pick you up in a heart beat. A girl could turn ten tricks in a few hours. Unfortunately, Jessy could never afford the ferry ride to get over there.

More bad luck.

"I have to go cop," she said. "I'll be back in a while."

More coughing, more blood. His nearly dead hand squeezed hers. "Make a wish first, just for fun."

Irritation was the only thing that could mask her sadness. "I'll tell you what I'd *like* to wish for," she spat. "A earthquake, right here. Split the Sound right open and suck everything down, the whole shitty city, all the people, everything. Fuck 'em."

"That's too hateful," he remarked. "You're not hateful. Make a real wish."

She wished they were dead. Her, Spad, the baby, all together. Painless. No more scabs, no more tricks, no more bridges. That's what she wished for. "There I've made it."

"So . . . what's your wish?"

"You're not supposed to tell!" she objected, "or it won't come true." Again, she wanted to look at him but couldn't. She wanted to kiss him. Couldn't.

She just kept looking at the sky, at the star. Two more appeared. Maybe this would be a meteor shower, like the ones she'd seen over the Chesapeake so long ago.

Finally, she asked him, "Did you make *your* wish?"

Spad didn't answer. His hand lay limp in hers; he was dead.

She refused to look at him. She should just get up and walk away and not look, because she didn't want to remember him that way. Looking would hurt too much, and she was sick of hurting. Silent tears shined on her cheeks. She felt short of breath, ripped off yet again by God or the universe or whatever.

The falling stars—three of them now—seemed to slow down. She didn't understand at first; usually falling stars disappeared in a wink, but these were arcing over the Sound in long glittery white streaks.

Jessy would have no reason to know what a MIRV was, or an air-burst proximity warhead. It occurred to her, though—in another second—that these weren't really falling stars. She gripped Spad's hand tighter. She had enough time to smile and feel warm. Then the sky turned white and her wish came true.

ABOUT THE AUTHOR

Edward Lee has authored close to 50 books in the field of horror; he specializes in hardcore fare. His most recent novels are LUCIFER'S LOTTERY and the Lovecraftian THE HAUNTER OF THE THRESHOLD. His movie HEADER was released on DVD by Synapse Film in June, 2009. Lee lives in Largo, Florida.

deadite press

"Brain Cheese Buffet" **Edward Lee** - collecting nine of Lee's most sought after tales of violence and body fluids. Featuring the Stoker nominated "Mr. Torso," the legendary gross-out piece "The Dritiphilist," the notorious "The McCrath Model SS40-C, Series S," and six more stories to test your gag reflex.

"Edward Lee's writing is fast and mean as a chain saw revved to full-tilt boogie."
- Jack Ketchum

"Bullet Through Your Face" **Edward Lee** - No writer is more extreme, perverted, or gross than Edward Lee. His world is one of psychopathic redneck rapists, sex addicted demons, and semen stealing aliens. Brace yourself, the king of splatterspunk is guaranteed to shock, offend, and make you laugh until you vomit.

"Lee pulls no punches."
- Fangoria

"Zombies and Shit" **Carlton Mellick III** - *Battle Royale* meets *Return of the Living Dead* in this post-apocalyptic action adventure. Twenty people wake to find themselves in a boarded-up building in the middle of the zombie wasteland. They soon realize they have been chosen as contestants on a popular reality show called Zombie Survival. Each contestant is given a backpack of supplies and a unique weapon. Their goal: be the first to make it through the zombie-plagued city to the pick-up zone alive. A campy, trashy, punk rock gore fest.

"Slaughterhouse High" **Robert Devereaux** - It's prom night in the Demented States of America. A place where schools are built with secret passageways, rebellious teens get zippers installed in their mouths and genitals, and once a year one couple is slaughtered and the bits of their bodies are kept as souvenirs. But something's gone terribly wrong when the secret killer starts claiming a far higher body count than usual . . .

"A major talent!" - Poppy Z. Brite

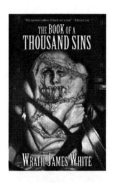

deadite press

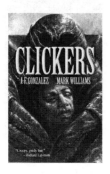

"Clickers" J. F. Gonzalez and Mark Williams- They are the Clickers, giant venomous blood-thirsty crabs from the depths of the sea. The only warning to their rampage of dismemberment and death is the terrible clicking of their claws. But these monsters aren't merely here to ravage and pillage. They are being driven onto land by fear. Something is hunting the Clickers. Something ancient and without mercy. *Clickers* is J. F. Gonzalez and Mark Williams' gore-soaked cult classic tribute to the giant monster B-movies of yesteryear.

"The Innswich Horror" Edward Lee - In July, 1939, antiquarian and H.P. Lovecraft aficionado, Foster Morley, takes a scenic bus tour through northern Massachusetts and finds Innswich Point. There far too many similarities between this fishing village and the fictional town of Love-craft's masterpiece, The Shadow Over Innsmouth. Join splatter king Edward Lee for a private tour of Innswich Point - a town founded on perversion, torture, and abominations from the sea.

"Urban Gothic" Brian Keene - When their car broke down in a dangerous inner-city neighborhood, Kerri and her friends thought they would find shelter inside an old, dark row home. They thought they would be safe there until help arrived. They were wrong. The residents who live down in the cellar and the tunnels beneath the city are far more dangerous than the streets outside, and they have a very special way of dealing with trespassers. Trapped in a world of darkness, populated by obscene abominations, they will have to fight back if they ever want to see the sun again.

"Jack's Magic Beans" Brian Keene - It happens in a split-second. One moment, customers are happily shopping in the Save-A-Lot grocery store. The next instant, they are transformed into bloodthirsty psychotics, interested only in slaughtering one another and committing unimaginably atrocious and frenzied acts of violent depravity. Deadite Press is proud to bring one of Brian Keene's bleakest and most violent novellas back into print once more. This edition also includes four bonus short stories:

"**Dead Bitch Army**" **Andre Duza** - Step into a world filled with racist teenagers, masked assassins, cannibals, a telekinetic hitman, 100 warped Uncle Sams, automobiles with razor-sharp teeth, living graffiti, cartoons that walk and talk, a steroid-addicted pro-athlete, an angry black chic, a washed-up Barbara Walters clone, the threat of a war to end all wars, and a pissed-off zombie bitch out for revenge.

"**Jesus Freaks**" **Andre Duza** - For God so loved the world that he gave his only two begotten sons… and a few million zombies. Thugs, pushers, gangsters, rapists, murderers; Detective Philip Makane thought he'd seen it all until he awoke on the morning of Easter Sunday 2015, to a world filled with bleeding rain, ravenous zombies, a homicidal ghost, and the sudden arrival of two men with extraordinary powers who both claim to be Jesus Christ in the flesh.

"**Trolley No. 1852**" **Edward Lee** - In 1934, horror writer H.P. Lovecraft is invited to write a story for a subversive underground magazine, all on the condition that a pseudonym will be used. The pay is lofty, and God knows, Lovecraft needs the money. There's just one catch. It has to be a pornographic story . . . The 1852 Club is a bordello unlike any other. Its women are the most beautiful and they will do anything. But there is something else going on at this sex club. In the back rooms monsters are performing vile acts on each other and doors to other dimensions are opening . . .

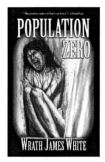

"**Population Zero**" **Wrath James White** - An intense sadistic tale of how one man will save the world through sterilization. *Population Zero* is the story of an environmental activist named Todd Hammerstein who is on a mission to save the planet. In just 50 years the population of the planet is expected to double. But not if Todd can help it. From Wrath James White, the celebrated master of sex and splatter, comes a tale of environmentalism, drugs, and genital mutilation.

AVAILABLE FROM AMAZON.COM

Lightning Source UK Ltd.
Milton Keynes UK
UKOW04f2215090414

229721UK00011B/270/P